DARK SHADOWS

I stood motionless, observing the harmonious rightness of the man in his natural habitat. My eyes followed the striding figure moving along the hillside path, and unconsciously I leaned farther and farther into the corner of the window to watch the man in secret.

The descending arc of the lantern flashed across my window and caught me full face, peering through the draperies. His arm paused so definitely I knew he'd seen me. I prayed he couldn't see me blush at being still awake when I'd long since said I was tired and should have been abed. The flickering light softened the rugged planes of his face, illumined the smile. I watched him retreat, and straightened the draperies slowly, wondering . . .

What was he doing here? And why did he wish that I had not come . . .

Elsie Lee

Mansion of Golden Windows

ZEBRA BOOKS
KENSINGTON PUBLISHING CORP.

ZEBRA BOOKS

are published by

Kensington Publishing Corp.
475 Park Avenue South
New York, NY 10016

First Zebra Books printing: June, 1988

Printed in the United States of America

Prologue

We have removed the crumbling stones of the fortalice. It would have cost more than sentiment is worth to reinforce and repair, even for a local landmark beloved by generations of tenantry. I am humbly grateful there was no word of protest when the Laird said it was not only dangerous, but too grim a reminder of terror and tragedy for his Lady.

"Aye, the puir bairn," the Town Council nodded gravely. "Take it doon, by a' means. . . ."

But, being Scots, they saved all the usable stones.

Some are set in the market square of Strathbogie, some are shoring up dilapidated pig sties or barns as far away as Oinsch, Kintore and Old Meldrum. The Great Cornerstone went, ceremoniously, to a museum in Edinburgh, and for weeks every antiquarian society in the British Isles photographed every conceivable angle.

We waited only long enough for Aunt Agnes to take a final look, but she went so ghastly pale, staring at the crenels, I feared a heart attack. "You—were up there, Sable?"

"Briefly, darling, but you can't kill a Lennox." I gently urged her away, back to the solarium, where she sank into a chair and closed her eyes with a sigh. The Laird swiftly produced a tot of brandy, and eventually she pulled herself together in a series of shakes, like a bird ruffling its feathers until they lie smooth to its satisfaction.

"It is entirely my fault, but since he didn't kill you, I needn't apologize." She tossed off the rest of her brandy and eyed the Laird militantly. "If you're really giving away the stones, I should like one."

"Have two," he countered blandly. "One for you, and one for a guest. . . ."

I look from the Strathmuir window, and the heather nearly covers the earth-fill of the keep beneath the fortalice. Sometimes I wonder if it was not some such human experiences that led Einstein to his theories of time. Definitely, it does go fast or slow, depending on what is occurring. It was a snail's pace while I hung from the crenel with only a toehold brace between me and a fifty-foot drop . . . yet now it rolls like a tumbleweed, and it is only by my son's staggering steps and warlike Scot shouts of joy that I know two years have passed.

Two years?

If I were a giant intellect (which God knows I am not), I would expand Einstein's theories by a formula to retard time, turn back the clock to moments one wants to keep forever. Then Aunt Agnes would be sitting here, braced on her goldheaded cane, contemplating the firefly lights, and smoking her after-dinner cigarette in the silent companionship we always shared. My husband says the formula I want *already exists.*

"It is in your mind, lass, and better so. You can recall selectively, and abandon the rest."

As always, he is right.

Amazing how quickly what is out of sight can be out of mind! The fortalice is gone; I no longer remember its appearance. I do not even bear a grudge against Annis for giving me the hot chocolate she must have known was lethal. But a dozen times a week I can close my eyes, hear Aunt Agnes's voice, imagine her next to me. How she'd have chortled over some of the local cases submitted to the Laird—like Steenie Cameron stating Elspie Morton's baby was her father's fault.

"He didna pay for ma bicycle, he's a'ready smashed it—I figured to get summat out o' the deal. . . ."

How she'd have browsed in the Record Room, because it was her passion for genealogy that began everything. It seems a pity she couldn't have had more years to enjoy her inadvertent contribution to the Family Tree—yet it if is true (as she believed) that each of us has a divinely ordained mission in life, hers was certainly fulfilled. . . .

Chapter 1

My name is Sable Lennox, because I was born prematurely during a Nova Scotia vacation. I expect I should be grateful; if I'd arrived respectably in Detroit, my name would have been Omega. After six previous babies, my parents hoped I'd be the last. Actually, I have twin younger brothers, which may prove that automotive engineers have a high octane rating all their own. The twins are Zed, and Zachary; after the mistake in my name, Mother took no chances.

I was a mistake in other ways, too. As a child, I was pugnacious, left-handed and tone-deaf. As an adult, I no longer blacken someone's eye when he disagrees, but I am still a misfit. I even look wrong. The others are either suave, sleek brunettes (Mother's Huguenot forebears), or pleasantly anomalous, with hair-colored hair and eye-colored eyes from Daddy's Anglo-Saxon heritage.

I am a Gordon Red.

My eyes are a clear, unmistakable green beneath a mop of red-blonde hair, and my skin is such that after five minutes in the sun I am pocked with freckles. Disgusting!

I was always pure Scot, the only one in the family who looked right in the dark green clan tartan. I was also my great-aunt's favorite. From the moment I grinned (a gas pain) at my godmother, we were *simpatico*. The rest of the family loved her dearly, and she heartily returned their affection—but Aunt Agnes and I were special.

We were Scots.

We *liked* bagpipes, porridge, fresh salmon and heather. We were *far*-sighted, artistic, nonarithmetical, addicted to word games and *views*. As a child, my greatest possible treat was sitting on her lap in the hideous old living room on Columbia Heights, watching Manhattan light up across the water. We were equally happy in the equally hideous Victorian summer home, contemplating assorted Berkshires. Despite a fifty-year age difference, we shared our interests—except that each of us had a quirk. Mine was preferring photography to painting in oils.

Aunt Agnes was hipped on genealogy.

She looked everyone up, and she kept the Family Tree. She spent years trying to prove Mother was related to Madame de Stael; and months on a possible connection to Montcalm. But she was best on Gordons. Aunt Agnes knew them backwards, forwards, upside-down to the most remote Setons, Richmonds, Lennoxes, *et al*.

When I was twelve, I drew the first family tree for her birthday present, on brown paper from the Chinese laundry. When Ling Wu understood I needed the paper for my ancestry, he gave me three yards and refused the dime I offered him. The colors were limited to my crayon set and a bit gaudy, but every entry was accurate.

I redrew it three times, until finally I put it on a window shade arrangement, scaled to fill the long living room wall. She could roll it up to the ceiling if she wanted to look at the Manets, Monets, Rembrandts and Renoirs Uncle Fred's sagacity had led him to buy on their Paris wedding trip in 1905.

Eventually, I became head of the photographic library for a major oil company. Aunt Agnes was sincerely proud when I won a few minor photographic awards, but aside from the pleasure of my company for dinner every Monday, the true value of having "Sable in New York" was to add new leaves and dates to The Tree. So I was not surprised to be summoned to a Friday dinner the instant she learned the oil company said I must either take all accumulated vacation next summer or forfeit the lot. It amounted to eight weeks; I would go abroad.

Walking down Clark Street, I wondered how she meant to con me into visiting Scotland. I didn't specially yearn for ancestral acres, but if it took no more than a week, I knew I'd do it.

"So you're going to Europe?" she said blandly.

"France, Italy—Spain, if there's time."

"Oh, there'll be plenty of time." Aunt Agnes hitched forward eagerly. "Now, Sable dear, what would you say to taking a few days to verify a couple of dates for me—and I'll give you the *whole* trip for a little present?"

I burst out laughing. "Oh Aunt Agnes, you darling old fraud! Of course I'll do what I can, and you will *not* give me any 'little present', sweetie. I've had the money for years, but not the time. What d'you want me to check?"

"I'll get it after dinner. I suppose," she sighed ruefully, "you think I'm an old fanatic—but it helps pass the time."

For a woman who never had to work and couldn't add two and two, her files were a miracle of organization! She hauled out a dozen folders from the study, gave me pad and pencil, pulled down the Family Tree and briskly set to work. "I got a lot when your Uncle Fred and I went to Huntly in 1928, the old Laird was most helpful—but the war changed things," she said grimly. "That damned Hitler managed to kill *everybody* from the male lines, Sable! And there were so many of 'em, I never kept as close track of the females. Now I have to fill gaps, because this new man has no son."

"Do you realize," she said impressively, "that it's possible *your* father, Charles Alexander Gordon-Lennox, might be the current heir?"

"Oh, dear, I hope not," I murmured uneasily. "I don't think he'd like it at all, Aunt Agnes."

"He wouldn't," she agreed, "but he'd do his duty, if required. I doubt it'll come to that." She scrabbled among the folders. "The descendants of Eleanor's younger daughters would take precedence."

(I'd better insert the basic family tree here.)

ALEXANDER SETON-GORDON (1690-1770)

Eleanor (1710)	James (1715)	George (1721)	Anne (1725)
Susan	Sandy	Charles	Died unwed
Chloe	Hamish	David	
Anne	Bettrys	Mary	
		Eliza	

There were other children, but only those four lived to maturity. The title went to James, descended to Sandy, who had no son, so it went sideways to Hamish. Around 1900, the Laird was a direct descendant of Hamish. He had four sons; there were plenty of other males, not only from the sons of the first Hamish, but also from the progeny of Charles and David. And then there were the wars—the First World War and the second World War, and by December 1943 all potential male heirs were gone.

This sent the entail back to the beginning again, for sons of sons from the eldest girl. Thus a direct male descendant from Eleanor's daughter Susan, preceded males from Chloe, etc. Aunt Agnes and Daddy were descended from Bettrys, and Mary and Eliza's descendants came last. "If it had to be that way, thank Heavens the old Laird outlived them," Aunt Agnes observed. "Only one set of death duties; he was at least able to keep Huntly and Strathmuir out of the Welsh coal revenues."

Her lips firmed austerely. "It's this David Kirby-Gordon I need to trace. His replies to my inquiries were so—politely repressive, I gave up, although everything's in the Huntly records. I simply hadn't enough time, so I concentrated on the male issues." She got to her feet, slowly crossed to the Family Tree, bracing herself on a chair and using the gold-headed cane to point. "See? The gaps are 1860 to 1900, Sable. Some things I remember: Susan's grandson was a David Kirby on Wellington's staff in the Peninsular Wars and killed at Bordeaux in 1814—but he'd married a Spanish gypsy who produced a son." Aunt Agnes chuckled drily as she hobbled back to her chair. "She brought him to Scotland, dumped him on the Clan and departed on the next Romany caravan passing through Strathbogie. It's in an old diary . . ."

"Gypsy blood? How titillating, better than a horse thief!"

"Entirely legitimate. Wellington himself witnessed the wedding. But Lord David prefers to forget this. Considering his parents, I'm not surprised."

"You *met* them?"

"I met her. George Kirby was killed in a street brawl," Aunt Agnes said. "She was chambermaid and he managed the racing stables for a fine English family. There was a shotgun wedding and he decamped. The employers saw her through for a while, but in 1928 she was a tearoom cashier in Liverpool." A picture plopped to the floor from her folder. Aunt Agnes studied it critically. "I'd forgotten I had that," she murmured, extending it. "Mary and George Kirby's wedding picture."

It was a garnish tint job. You could see the Rom in him: black eyes and hair, Slavic bones, a sense of neither to hold nor to bind . . . irresistible to the weak-

14

chinned girl smiling happily nestled within his arms. I thought the masses of waving dull blonde hair, soft eyes and plump bosom were probably equally irresistible to George Kirby. "What happened to her?"

"Coventry raid," Aunt Agnes shrugged. She replaced the picture and continued her instructions to me. I ended with five pages of notes—and an unexplained deposit of $5,000 to my checking account.

"What's this for?"

"Rent a car and drive to Scotland."

"Dammit, I can afford that on my own."

She was unexpectedly serious. "You may have to stay in lodgings at Strathbogie, or drive from one place to another. I've written the Laird saying what I want and asking permission for you to use family records, but I'm not sure he'll grant it, Sable."

"How could he refuse?"

"He's the Laird, it's his right to be private even from a Clan member," she said, "and if the line could disintegrate to the son of a chambermaid, he may not wish the records to be too accurate," she added drily. "Remember, he isn't a gentleman by our standards!"

I scanned my notes. There seemed nothing to produce problems. Two days should do it for a woman accustomed to the use of files. I had my mouth open to say so, when I realized Aunt Agnes's face was grim. "What troubles you, darling?"

"I don't know," she murmured, shaking her head helplessly, "except that—I don't like the smell of it." She thrust two envelopes at me. "Promise me, you'll present both of these *before* you go to Scotland."

I read two names: Lord Everard Campbell, Lord Lieutenant and Chief Constable, Cascadine, Aberdeenshire; and John Morrisy, Chief, C.I.D., Scotland Yard. I gulped. "Aunt Agnes, why would I need Scotland Yard?"

"I don't know," she said again, "but Margaret, the old Laird's youngest sister, lived to meet David Kirby-Gordon. She didn't like him, Sable." Aunt Agnes looked at me earnestly. "She couldn't explain. I can't either, but from his original letters I knew what she meant.

"D'you see, he doesn't have to care about the Clan genealogy. You don't either, really—but you're aware of it. Somehow, he wasn't. Margaret said it was more than being an uneducated commoner; it was as if he didn't belong at all, and didn't care to belong. He was trying to adapt, but it was unconvincing, mere lip service." Aunt Agnes's eyes met mine compellingly.

"You're to present both letters," she said quietly. "You're to see how the land lies. But if there's the least difficulty, you're to come away at once. Promise me. . . ."

"What sort of difficulty?" I asked, bewildered.

"Promise me!" she repeated stubbornly. "He may be different after twenty years as Laird, but no matter what he says or does, Sable—*remember he is not a gentleman."*

Chapter 2

Call me a Sassenach, but I loved England, beginning with John Morrisy, who was grizzled, keen-eyed, soft-spoken. "Aunt Agnes *would* have me get in touch with you," I told him, "but I won't apologize, because it's a thrill to meet the prototype of M!"

He raised a shaggy eyebrow. "M indeed! Good God, will we ever live down James Bond?" he snorted. When we'd finished laughing, he asked, "Why *did* she want you to get in touch with us?"

"I don't know. She says she doesn't either, except she has a *feeling* . . . that the Laird may be unpleasant over any digging into family archives, if he permits it at all, because 'Lord David is not a gentleman.'" I grinned at Morrisy. "I refrained from telling Aunt Agnes the harsh truth that, by her standards, few men are these days. It was immensely kind of you to see me, Inspector Morrisy, but I know how busy you are . . ."

"Not so fast, young lady," he made notes, ignoring a buzz that stopped so abruptly I knew a secretary had got it. "In the first place, my wife will want to meet you,

17

and in the second place, Agnes Ware is not given to fantasies. If she thinks you need the protection of Scotland Yard, even if she can't explain why, I'll take her word for it." He smiled, stood up to extend his hand. "Dinner tomorrow night?"

London was wonderful, Ascot a thrill, and under the aegis of the Chief of Scotland Yard, I was presented to Her Majesty! Mrs. Morrisy was a bubbling Irish woman who took one look at me and said, "Saints preserve us, you're the image of Mrs. Ware! A beauty she was, and you are, too . . . how well I remember her. We were just-married. John had just been made Assistant to the Chief, who was friend to Mr. Ware." She chuckled richly. "We're summoned to dine. I'd no formal dress to me name, but I'd a sewing machine and the living room draperies just completed. . . . That proud I was—but I took 'em down, ripped 'em apart, and used the lining for me dinner gown."

I stayed on in London photographing everything: Covent Garden, Temple Inns, Cheyne Walk, Wimpole Street. I rode to the end of every omnibus line. Eileen Morrisy went along "for the ride. The things ye know about this city! This Pendennis and Becky Sharp, now—would they be real or fancy?"

"Only people in books, I'm sorry . . ."

"Oh, don't apologize, macushla, it's a new London I'm seeing. . . ."

I'd written a short note to Lord David Kirby-Gordon, saying I was in London and planned to drive north. I hoped he'd permit me to check a few family dates in the Huntly records. I had a formal reply: the

Laird was in Wales but would be happy to meet an American clanswoman. It was signed, "Sincerely, Annis Kirby-Gordon."

I showed it to John Morrisy. "She sounds receptive," I said.

"Yes," he agreed. "There seems nothing against the Laird, Sable. He's not precisely liked in the shire, but he's accepted socially . . . had the sense to leave estate management to a cousin, admits he doesn't understand land, and prefers business. There's no doubt he's increased the family assets handsomely." He cleared his throat uneasily. "I can't put my finger on anything," he said flatly, "aside from mistrust of an outlander."

"Shouldn't that be gone, after twenty years?"

Morrisy nodded. "I told Lord Everard you'd telephone when you reached Scotland; he wants you to spend the night at Cascadine."

I rented an Austin-Healey, detoured south to Stonehenge, north to Oxford, worked slowly up to Nottingham, detoured again to the Cumbrians, savoring the Yorkshire accent and place names: Scafell, Skiddaw, Wigton, Askrigg. Miraculously, the weather was unbroken—not always sun, but never rain. Nightly I despatched film to the London developer, and finally I was through the Cheviots, entering Edinburgh.

Oddly, I wasn't thrilled; I liked England better—but I didn't say so in the diary. Aunt Agnes had given me a big fat book bound in flamingo pink leather with lock and key, "so you needn't bother with lettars. Send a postcard now and then."

"Did you *have* to get such a nauseating color?"

"Yes, I had," Aunt Agnes said firmly. "It was the only one fat enough, and don't tell me you're an artist, not a novelist. You'll find plenty to fill it."

She was right. The diary was practically filled when I phoned Lord Everard Campbell. His voice had a pleasant burr, giving directions for roads to Cascadine. "Ye'll nae reach us afore sundoon, but we're detairmined to keep ye a few days, so press yersel', lass." I stopped only long enough to buy another fat diary in Edinburgh. Once away from the city, I began to enjoy Scotland . . . stopping occasionally for pictures here and there. It was nearly seven before I braked in front of a low rambling country house that was warm with lights, and before I'd time even to draw breath, the front door was flung wide. Silhouetted against the light was a stocky male figure, brave in a kilt. He switched on entrance lamps and hobbled forward eagerly while a tiny woman appeared behind him, waiting in the doorway.

Anyone who thinks the Scots are reserved should meet Lord Everard and Lady Jean. Granted, my welcome was mostly for Aunt Agnes, but in two minutes, I was gleefully dragged from the car, into the house, soundly bussed by both host and hostess, and provided with a wee drappie. An efficient manservant had taken my luggage upstairs, a beaming fresh-faced maid trotted in with a bowl of ice for the American guest, and the faint but succulent odor of roast mutton tickled my nose.

I looked at the Campbells, raised my glass and said, earnestly, "I apologize for everything I ever said or thought about genealogy. Please—we're related?"

"I'm afraid not," Lord Everard chuckled. "In fact,

we're hereditary enemies. You Gordons! Och, ye're a turbulent lot!"

"Oh, dear, I'm afraid you're right—but no matter what Aunt Agnes wrote you, I haven't bashed anyone since I was ten."

I'd have been perfectly happy to go no farther than Cascadine. If I'd liked the Morrisys, I loved the Campbells: Lord Everard, seventy-ish and a bit lame, but still sturdy enough to exhaust me in a hike along the howe or into a glen—and Lady Jean, who watched birds, fussed over her superb rock garden and knitted socks for her husband. They adopted me whole-heartedly, petted me like a granddaughter, and were so obviously enjoying a young guest that I hated to leave, but I had been invited to stay at Strathmuir by Lord David Kirby-Gordon!

Even as I accepted the phoned invitation, I had a snide suspicion it was offered only because I was staying with the Lord Lieutenant of the shire. I'd first thought the Laird meant to reverse his wife's permission to use clan records, but at mention of Cascadine, he became extremely affable. I was increasingly reluctant. But it'd be twice as quick to get what Aunt Agnes wanted if I were in the house. . . .

"I had no intention of imposing on you beyond access to the records, but if it's really not inconvenient, I'd like very much to visit."

"Splendid, splendid! When would you like to come, Miss Lennox?"

"I'd planned to drive to Strathbogie tomorrow, but perhaps that's too short notice."

21

"Not at all, not at all. Market day, some of us would be in town anyway. If you'll drive to the White Hart, someone will meet you—easier than trying to give directions. The road out of town is confusing. No trouble at all. We look forward to it."

I couldn't feel equal anticipation. The longer he talked, the more cordial his voice, the less impressed I was.

"What's he like?" I asked Lord Everard bluntly.

"We've only met a few times on the Bench, once or twice in company," he said slowly. "Younger than we, not in the same circles—not sure I can tell ye, Sable."

"Well, I can," his wife broke in decidedly. "The man's a bounder, who stole his cousin's sweetheart to help him make a good impression—not that I've any use for Annis Richmond. She loves only her comfort, and Sholto was well rid of her. She waited long enough to be certain he'd not be Laird, and off she went to the altar with the moneybags. Hmph, I'll be bound she paid dear for a commoner who had to be taught which fork to use! Yon's an oily conniver, Sable, wi' damp hands."

"Miss Lennox?"

"Yes . . ."

"I'm Sholto Comyn. The Laird asked me to show you the road to Strathmuir."

The man standing before my table in the taproom was the apotheosis of dark Highland Scot, from wavy thick black hair to compact sinewy body and hawk-eyes of an incredibly deep sapphire blue, rimmed by long black lashes. I held out my hand. "How d'you do? Must

22

we leave at once, or will you join me for a drink?"

His handshake was brusque but not damp. He eyed my barely tasted highball with disfavor. "Ye'll not wish to waste it. Tam, bring me the same." Unsmiling, he sat across from me, looking silently about, while the bartender fixed the drink and I stared at Sholto's averted face.

Well! Nothing could have been plainer! Now I knew the meaning of *dour,* but why should he so dislike me on sight? Was this the treatment I'd get from the Laird and Lady Annis? Then why had I been invited? By the time Tam sat the glass on the table, the Gordon Red temper was stirring.

Sholto picked up the drink and said, "I hope you had a good trip, Miss Lennox."

"Very pleasant," I returned, deliberately, "until now." His eyes widened over the rim of the glass. "Why d'you wish I hadn't come, Mr. Comyn?"

"Lord Aboyne," he murmured automatically, "and it's no concern of mine how many little spinsters wish to trace their ancestors." He drained his glass. "If you're finished, Miss Lennox?"

"Not quite. Does Lord David share your contempt for genealogy, because I'd be happy to stay here as originally planned. I shouldn't like the Laird to feel he *must* invite me as a guest, merely because I'm distantly related—or even open the Huntly records if he'd rather not. I assure you I'm not an 'ugly American' riding roughshod over local customs."

"No, you're far from ugly," he agreed. "Hereabouts your face would be your passport, aside from the name. You're a true Gordon Red, even to the green eyes."

I could feel myself blushing furiously at the faint twitch of his lips, and became madder than ever. "Do I stay—or do I respect his privacy and go back to Lord Everard Campbell tonight?"

"Everard?" His face was amazingly transformed by affection. He was almost handsome when he smiled. "He's my godfather—and ye've come from Cascadine this day? How are they?"

"Well and happy. They're friends of my godmother. Once I'm finished here, I'm to spend a fortnight with them before I go to France. If I ever get there. They're such darlings one can't bear to leave. Now will you please answer my question, Lord Aboyne?"

"O'course ye'll stay till your work's done. Come along, lass." He stood up, smiling ruefully. "I'll apologize for my foul temper. You've only the Gordon, but I've the Aboyne bad humor as well—and it was a tiresome day. I'm longing for a bath and a drink, but I've to wait about for an American girl and see her safe to Strathmuir." He shrugged. "If ye're a real Gordon, ye'll understand—and pardon me."

I laughed helplessly at the teasing twinkle. "It doesn't require a Gordon, only a woman," I assured him, gathering purse and gloves together. "I'm sorry I delayed your bath, but at least you've had a drink."

There was a slight crisis when he expected to drive and I wouldn't surrender the ignition key. "I won't remember the turns or forks unless I *do* them—or did you plan to chauffeur me every day?"

"No woman drives while a man sits."

"You should come to America, Lord Aboyne, the men have really got it made over there," I told him sweetly. "If you'll feel too deeply humiliated, tell me

24

how to get out of Strathbogie, and you can squat on the floor so no one will recognize you."

He glared at me, but I glared right back. After a while he got sulkily into the car, slamming the door with unnecessary force. I slid behind the wheel, adjusted the driving pillow and started the engine. "Which way?"

"Straight ahead."

By the time we reached Strathmuir, I could agree that it'd be nearly impossible to give directions over a telephone. You could *see* the place, sitting on a hill overlooking town and rivers, but getting to it was another matter. We went right, we went left, we crossed the Bogie once and the Deveron twice; we went around a couple of small hills and over another, while Sholto sat in disapproving silence, saying "left at the fork," or "straight through." We met a few cars and passed some farm wains drawn by plodding horses, and suddenly I could see the fortalice behind the main house.

Not that I knew what it was, then. It was only a stone tower, stark against the twilight sky, with crumbling crenels. "What's that?"

"The remains of a Comyn fortalice."

As if *that* explained everything! I was sufficiently annoyed that I wouldn't ask for more. Finally we were across a sort of dry moat, into a bumpy cobbled court, drawing to a stop before shallow stone steps and a great wooden double door that was partly open. Sholto got out of the car and gave a peculiar yell that nearly split my ears. "EeeeeeooooooHHHHEEEEEEEE." Then he stalked around to open my door.

"What was *that* in aid of?" I asked dazedly. "Don't tell me you cherish a secret passion for cowboys and

25

Indians on the Late Show?"

"Ye dinna ken the Clan cry?" he returned sardonically, speaking with a broad Scottish burr for the first time. "Och, weel, it appears ye've more to lairn than whaur ye cam' from, lassie."

"I know where I came from, thank you, which is more than I can say for you," I said spiritedly. "African gorilla forebears, I shouldn't wonder."

He put hands on hips, threw back his head and guffawed. Lights sprang up in the door lanterns and a butler trotted down the steps. "Good evening, Milord—Miss Lennox." He swiftly transferred luggage to the hall as Sholto continued laughing. I had a flashing memory of the Family Tree. Oh, heavens, he wasn't just a lord—he was both the Earl of Aboyne and the Earl of Sutherland and I was sassing him?

"Miss Lennox—*cousin,*" he said softly, still chuckling, "in one sentence you have illumined the entire Colonial Revolt for me. I'll wager Bettrys Gordon-Lennox started the Boston Tea Party, judging by the temper of her descendant. Gorillas, indeed!" His hand caught my elbow, turned me toward the entrance doors before I could find my voice.

Fleetingly I wondered, since he was so contemptuous of genealogy, how he knew I was on the Bettrys line? Then we were in a square hall, facing a polite elderly housekeeper. "Here is Mrs. Frame, to show you to your room, Miss Lennox—and Andrew's already taken your bags." I could see the butler disappearing at the top of the stairs while I smiled at Mrs. Frame and automatically followed her.

Halfway up the stairs I leaned over the handrail. Sholto'd lit a cigarette and under the lovely old crystal chandelier his dark blue eyes were inscrutable, masked in a cloud of drifting smoke. "Oh—thank you so much for showing me the way, Lord Aboyne, and I'm sorry I was snippy. Forgive, please?"

"Tchk, think shame to yersel', lass," he said instructively. "A Gordon never apologizes, never retreats. I can see the bluid line has weakened in the past centuries." He grinned up at me wickedly. "Och, weel, for a woman ye're no' too bad a driver," he said generously and sketched a polite bow. "Till we meet again, Miss Lennox—cousin."

A pleasant chambermaid said, "The Laird's compliments, and the family assembles in the solarium for drinks before dinner. I'm Nellie, miss, to show you the way." By her approving glance, I gathered I looked okay. Lady Jean had warned me to expect formality— "Dresses every night, kilts and the dining room pipes. He's verra traditional," she'd sniffed. "He doesna dare be otherwise."

I picked up the soft woolen evening stole I'd already learned one needs anywhere in the British Isles, even in summer, and followed Nellie. The house was all ups and downs, transverse halls and angular turns before one finally emerged at the top of the main stairs. I wondered how old it was, how many times expanded to suit the whim of some former Laird. And yet it had every modern convenience of electricity, hot water, modern plumbing.

Now that I was about to meet the Clan Laird, I was unexpectedly nervous. All responsibility for representing the American branch rested on me, particularly for

Aunt Agnes's sake. Nellie pushed back a door, "Miss Lennox, milord," and I faced a man, springing to his feet and coming toward me, while a woman leaned forward in her chair politely.

Lord David Kirby-Gordon was a medium man: height, bones, coloring. He was faintly sharpfaced despite the cordial smile, cold light-gray eyes beneath sparse eyebrows and sandy-gray hair. I'd have thought him a good ten years older than his age, which I knew to be forty-six—but a war veteran might be prematurely aged.

"Miss Lennox, welcome, welcome—come in, come in!" Lady Jean was right: his handshake *was* damp. He drew me forward. "Let me present you to my wife. Annis, here is our American cousin, Miss Lennox."

She was a scraggy woman with faded blue eyes and a fashionable hairdo that only emphasized gold-tinted hair. She once must have been extremely pretty, but it was only a memory, which might explain the discontented lines about her mouth. She extended a limp hand and said, "Delighted to meet you, Miss Lennox."

But she wasn't; she wished that I hadn't come. Then why had she answered my London letter, giving me permission to use the records? I sat very erect in the chair Lord David had indicated, and I thought: Lady Annis couldn't wish me away any more than I do, right now!

The Laird was unimpressive, over-eager in preparing my highball, ingratiating as a dog hoping for a pat on the head. Nervous, wary—that accounted for the perspiring hands. "You had a comfortable trip? How are the Campbells? Delightful people!"

"Aren't they? Both well, and send their respects to

you. I'm to return for a few weeks when I've finished here."

"You mustn't hurry away, Miss Lennox! We mean to keep you as long as we can. Not every day we've a chance to meet an American cousin!"

"Too kind of you, but my time is limited . . ."

"Good evening, Annis . . . David—sorry to be delayed, but the telephone caught me as I was leaving my room." Sholto, Earl of Aboyne and Sutherland, bent to kiss Annis's hand. "Miss Lennox, good evening to you."

His entrance changed the atmosphere. Annis seemed to relax slightly. The Laird's light eyes slitted briefly, then he was jovially pressing Sholto to fix a drink. I sat back in my chair observing the scene: two men in dinner jackets and formal kilts—and Sholto's, whether Aboyne or Sutherland, was one of the gaudy plaids, yet anyone would have known at once he was the born aristocrat, while the Laird o'Gordon looked like a Flushing haberdasher going to a fancy dress party.

"Miss Lennox—cousin, ye're verra silent," Sholto's deep Scottish burr crooned. "Summat amiss, ye're o'ertired by the drive?"

"That little bitty stuff and nonsense?" I widened my eyes, amazed. "If it's roads ye want, Lord Aboyne, ye must come to the States: the Mohawk Trail, Blue Ridge, Ozarks, Appalachians—and that's nothing compared to the Mojave, the Sierra Madres or the Everglades. Och, cousin, ye've nothing here to daunt a Colonial."

"Is it still so wild then?" Annis murmured, surprised.

The Laird snorted impatiently. "Of course not, Annis! The States are as civilized as anything here, if

29

not more so."

Her thin lips tightened mutinously. "Why so crushing over an innocent question? You've never been there, after all."

"You're both right, actually," I injected. "Our big cities are like yours—London, Edinburgh, and the rest—but because we have so much land, there's an immense amount we haven't needed to use so far . . . not wild or dangerous, but simply natural and unspoiled. I remember Her Majesty said, the first time she went to Canada, she thought she'd never get to the end of it. Anyway, once you come to the States, you'll understand," I said. "Why don't you come? There's a sizable body of clansmen who'd be happy to greet you."

The Laird was smiling again. "You make it very alluring, Miss Lennox. Annis, shall we go and see for ourselves?"

"If you wish, David."

From the far end of the immense stone fire mantel, Sholto's deep eyes regarded me impassively. "We've wandered from the initial question," he remarked. "If not tired, why so quiet, cousin?"

"I was considering how best to photograph you," I squinted, tilting my head. "The Laird slightly right center, his hand resting on the mantel—you as you are, Lord Aboyne, a bit in the shadows and facing straight ahead, your shoulders leaning against the stones, one leg half-bent, at ease . . . 21 mm, f.4 wide angle, Kodachrome II . . . pity I haven't the lights." I glanced about regretfully. "And you've nothing suitable, or we'd have a superb family portrait. With Lady Annis in a soft pink gown"—I squinted again, creating the picture in my mind—"seated on that ottoman between

30

you, looking a bit to the left. Her gold hair and the soft pink gown would bridge from the dark tartan to the bright, d'you see?" Lost in the composition, I'd completely forgotten Lady Jean's words: *He's a bounder who stole his cousin's sweetheart.* . . .

The butler's voice said, "The Laird is served."

We finished our drinks, stood up, and most correctly, the Laird offered his arm to me. I felt barely able to totter. Of all *gaffes* I could have made, what could be worse? What to say? "I cannot thank you enough for permitting me to use the records, Lord David."

"Now, now, no formality needed." He held the chair to his right. "My name is David to any clanswoman."

I smiled feebly and sat down facing Sholto. Damn the man, *he'd* caused me to put my foot into it. "How kind of you, David," I purred. "My friends call me Sable."

"Sable?" Annis repeated. "So unusual. A family name?"

"A whim of my great-aunt's. I was born in Nova Scotia."

David looked up brightly. "You were named for Cape Sable? Charming!" He doused oil on his smoked salmon slices, neatly cut apart and wrapped about a teaspoon of capers. "Great-aunt. That would be Mrs. Ware? Tell me about her."

"She's Mrs. Frederick Ware, and in America that says it." I took a bit of my salmon and suppressed a growl of satisfaction: *not* obtainable Stateside, even at caviar prices.

"At the risk of insularity, this is *not* America," Sholto observed. "Who is Mrs. Frederick Ware, aside

31

from your great-aunt and a member of the clan?"

"Agnes Seton, father's aunt, my godmother, about eighty years old," I said, "and between Texas oil wells and Canadian goldfields, plus Uncle Fred's sagacity in 1929, she's so filthy rich she doesn't miss the income tax."

There was a slight silence. "A provocative statement, cousin," Sholto murmured. "Tell us more." His eyes held a sardonic gleam, but I sensed David and Annis pricking up their ears. So they thought Aunt Agnes only a silly old nuisance? I'd bet the local banker knew the Ware name. Hah, I'd tell them how they'd missed the boat!

"Well, she's so outrageously rich, there's nothing to do but laugh about it," I said casually. "Father says Congress makes an annual pool on how much she'll pay, and whoever comes closest gets to use the money for his pet project. The first major appropriation after tax day we ask, 'Did you see what you built this year?' At home we call Hoover Dam, the Tennessee Valley Authority and *all* of NASA 'Aunt Aggie's civic good works,' but we love her anyway."

Sholto chuckled irrepressibly, but Annis was rigid with incredulity. "Doesn't she *object?*"

I looked at her humorless eyes and abandoned all thought of good impressions. "Only the year father said she was responsible for continuance of meat rationing, because if she'd paid more the year before, the government could have stock-piled beef."

"Oh, Sable—cousin," Sholto choked, "what did she say? I already know she had the last word."

"Of course. She said it wasn't her fault, but daddy's. That was the year the twins were born, and after she'd

32

given them the usual trust fund, there wasn't enough for steaks." I finished the last crumb of salmon and wiped my mouth. "I was ten, so I remember. It was at dinner and my sister Chloe had said why was it always chickens that weren't rationed? If she had to eat many more, she'd forget how to talk and start clucking. Then father sassed Aunt Agnes"—I'd forgotten my audience and unconsciously mimicked Aunt Agnes's austere voice—"and she said, 'Little did I think, Charles, when I offered a trust fund for your first child that your wife planned a private population explosion; but if steaks ye must have, toss a coin, take either, Zed or Zachary, stuff an apple in his mouth, and the survivor gets all.'"

Sholto was wiping his eyes with his napkin, laughing in a series of snorts. David smiled easily. "How much I'd like to meet her! I'd no idea Mrs. Ware was a financier—but you say she's eighty? Does she manage her own affairs?"

I shook my head. "She can't add two and two. There's a battery of business advisers, mostly sons or grandsons of Uncle Fred's partners."

"He was in—trade?" Annis asked.

"About like David," I returned sweetly. "Uncle Fred inherited a packet. He never needed to work, but it amused him to encourage new enterprise, like AT&T, IBM, General Motors, Anaconda Copper, Noranda. . . ."

Bouillon replaced the appetizer. I picked up my spoon and noted Lord Aboyne sitting tightlipped, staring at me contemptuously before he bent to his own soup. *What the hell's wrong with him?* I wondered dazedly.

"Does Mrs. Ware still back new developments?"

Something in David's tone spelled caution. "I've no idea, I'm not privy to her financial affairs, David." I smiled at Annis. "Delicious broth! You grow your own herbs?"

"Such as will survive. I've only a forcing frame."

"Basil, sage and marjoram," I nodded. "You do need temperature control for cumin or fenugreek." It was the first spark I'd struck.

"You've grown herbs, Sable? I thought you lived in the city."

"I do, but Aunt Agnes went in for gastronomy a while back. She imported everything: nutmeg, cinnamon, saffron, even a clove tree—but either we have the wrong kind of bees in the Berkshires, or the trees were unhappy so far from home, because they all died. After that she went in for genealogy." I smiled limpidly at Sholto. "She's the one who's interested in family lineage because she never had any children," I murmured. "But we think it's better than endowing a home for cats or starting a new religion."

"Definitely. Do I gather you don't share her passion?"

"Not in the least. I don't care where I came from, so long as I'm here."

"Does Mrs. Ware know that?" David asked, with the sly smile that invites conspiracy. *Yon's an oily conniver.* . . .

I exaggerated amazement. "Of course—just as I know she's not interested in photography."

"So you're a professional photographer," Sholto said. "We should have guessed! David, I think we must find the proper lights and cajole our cousin into that family portrait. I've an idea a Lennox is already the

34

equal of a Beaton."

"D'you have a studio, then? Have you had a personal show?"

"Only competition entries so far, Annis. I haven't much time. I'm head of the photographic library of an oil company. I expect you'd say I'm in trade."

"You work?" Annis was bewildered. "I thought you have a private income from Mrs. Ware."

"I do." I let it lie there, while cups were exchanged for fish plates. Good heavens, was it a Lillian Russell-Diamond Jim Brady type dinner—or was this the main dish? No, no vegetables. Did they eat this way every night, or was it to impress a visitor? They were cleaning their plates *d'habitude*. Where did they put so much food? None of them was fat. Annis was downright bony. David a bit sagged and pouched, but Sholto was all muscle and energy.

I took one bit of the turbot soufflé with cream sauce, sipped the wine Andrew had poured, closed my eyes and apologized to God and the starving babies of the world, then deliberately messed up the remainder. While Sholto was talking to David, I turned to Annis. "Your daughters are at school?"

"Elizabeth's first year at Newnham," she nodded. "Sisley's at St. Hilda's, two more years."

"I'm sorry not to meet them. I expect you're anxious to have them home for the long vac?"

"Yes and no," she sighed. "We were going abroad, David *promised,* and now he says he can't get away after all. I must either go alone again, or make do with a week in the Orkneys as usual. It's too provoking of him! Considering he's never been anywhere except a few months when he was wounded at Anzio, I don't understand his lack of interest. Not as if we'd go to Italy—I'll concede he mightn't want to see where he lost his hand, but France . . . or Norway?"

"Lost his hand?" I lowered my voice and glanced at the Laird. He was left-handed, I'd already seen that much, but the right hand seemed normal flesh and bone.

"Figuratively," she said. "He was shot in the right arm. They put it back after a fashion, but it's still stiff. *Months* of retraining before he could use the left hand. That was particularly difficult because he'd just become Laird—and couldn't sign anything. Every time we had to use *two* witnesses while he made an X—so many older tenants can't write, you know. So it had to be me and the minister or a lawyer, but with petrol rationing I couldn't drive from Rhynie everyday. . . ."

I was listening with only half an ear, my eyes were fixed on the Laird's hands . . . deftly finishing his fish, raising the wine glass, absently fingering the stem with his left, while his right lay in his lap.

Perhaps it had taken months of retraining; perhaps in twenty years it had become natural. But I was a *natural* southpaw, and I felt positive that David Kirby-Gordon had always been left-handed, too.

Chapter 3

Did I look too long, too fixedly at those hands—or did my face reveal bewilderment? As the plates were changed, my eyes met Sholto's. His expression was still grimly impersonal, yet I felt he'd caught my scrutiny of David's hands. . . . I had the curious impression he wished to prevent any deeper consideration of them. "Tell us about your work, cousin Sable."

"I get packets of photographs from all over the world, to be indexed, cross-indexed, filed, sometimes copied innumerable times, occasionally discarded as worthless. I—it's rather fascinating to me."

"Why should an oil company want photographs?" Annis asked.

"Endless reasons, Annis, mostly too technical to interest you. But the field men not only take the required pictures of terrain or installations, they're shutterbugs on the side. They photograph natives, tribal dances, scenic wonders, kids at local schools. Do you know," I looked at David seriously, "*one* roll of film—thirty-six pictures of an African village—

brought a representative of UNICEF and a team from the Peace Corps to upper Dahomey in *two days!*"

"There's oil in Dahomey?" the Laird asked.

"Not a drop." I looked at his sharp rat-face and suddenly hated him. *Anyone* should have wanted to know how and why, appreciated the wily way we'd got those pictures into the UN for action—but all David Kirby-Gordon, son of a chambermaid, asked about was oil. . . .

I was saved by the pipes. From the service door emerged a ceremonial pageant: Andrew, bearing an immense roast of beef, followed by two serving maids carrying vegetable dishes, with a maid at the rear burdened with hot rolls, relishes and condiments.

Most impressive. As the door swung back, it was kicked open again, and the pipes entered: three stalwart lads in the clan tartan, skirling full blast. Thrice about the table they went while the Laird neatly sliced the beef, setting pieces onto a hot platter, which Andrew picked up with serving mitts. I gave him a gold star for being observant: he'd already realized I was left-handed and was serving me from the right.

Beef, roasted potatoes, new peas, Yorkshire pudding, English mustard, a gravy boat, currant jelly, hot rolls, more butter—and behind the Laird the pipes lined up, still skirling briskly. David's jaw tensed as he served himself from platter and dishes.

Well, not everyone enjoys the squeal of a bagpipe, but I never knew a Scot who couldn't take it. Annis was calm, no more aware than the owner of a grandfather clock is of its hourly chimes. Sholto was, if anything, sitting straighter, his lips pursed and barely restrained from whistling as he delicately forked through the beef slices to find one that was reasonably rare. I looked at David's choice of overdone outside slice.

As the final squeal of "Captain Car" died away, I exclaimed wide-eyed, "Oh, David—so wonderful! Could they do 'Adam o'Gordon'?"

"Aye, that we can, mistress," the First Pipe beamed—and in a twinkling they were stepping, prancing about the table, while I let my beef grow cold for the pleasure of the pipes. By the time they'd surrounded the Laird's chair, with the final expiring sigh in his ear, David was ready to faint. He gave me no chance for another request. "Thank you, thank you, that's enough, Steenie, we'd like to talk."

I caught Steenie looking disconcerted at the curt dismissal and said: "'Twas aye wunnerful for an outlander who loves her music but canna speak her language properly, ye'll pardon ma ignorance?"

His face cleared. "'Tis good to meet a clanswoman wha kens her music, mistress." Bobbing, grinning, the pipers disappeared, leaving silence behind, until Sholto rescued me by a casual remark on local affairs that created chit-chat. I ate my beef quietly; there was no salad. For dessert there was a *flan,* which seems ubiquitous in the British Isles.

What it *is,* is a sort of crusty half circle of dough filled with custard and topped with whatever fruit or preserves are on hand. The custard is made out of a powder packet, and if you're lucky, the topping *may* be Cooper's Oxford. After a few bouts with an English *flan*, you will never again snigger at Betty Crocker.

"Sable, you've eaten so little—was something not to your taste?"

"Not at all, David, everything was delicious—but so

much driving, such a long day, I'm afraid I'm a bit tired."

"Of course, of course! Sleep till you wake! When ever you're ready, I'll take you to the record room and explain the filing system. Although," David smiled heartily, "I imagine you know more than I."

"Files, yes—genealogy, no! Why, Sholto knows more than I, for all he's so supercilious about lineage."

"Oh, I'll never live it down, will I?" he laughed, glancing at the Laird. "I called her a little spinster, but when I gave the Clan yell to summon Andrew, she had the last word. She asked if my ancestors were gorillas."

Annis looked a bit shocked. "Do you know *nothing* of the relationships of the Clan, Sable?"

"One gets a bit confused by the fourteenth-century bastards," I apologized. "Nearly as bad as the Genesis begattings, except our family names are less pronounceable."

"Ye're going back to Jock o'Scurdargue and Tam o'Ruthven?" Sholto inquired. "Lord, that'll take ye all summer, cousin!"

"Yes, it was a good day for genealogists when John Knox invented hell-fire for Scotland so people had to get married," I agreed, "but all Aunt Agnes wants is 1860 to 1910."

"She already *has* the bastard lines?" he asked irrepressibly.

"Oh, nonsense!" the Laird smiled at me, pushing back from the table. "You mustn't heed Sholto's sense of humor, Sable."

"It *is* more than one expects from a gorilla," I murmured, smiling at Lord Aboyne, while Annis frowned slightly.

"You're just joking, surely, Sable?"

"Yes, she's joking, Annis." Sholto gently assisted her to her feet, while the Laird escorted me back to the solarium.

"1860 to 1910? I'll admit I never explored family records, but I know they were fully maintained from about 1830," he was saying. I had an odd impression of inner tension relaxed, as he settled me in a chair and sank into his own. While Annis and Sholto entered, Andrew produced a coffee tray equipped with liqueurs.

"Do you have a librarian?" I asked politely.

"Not necessary. The old Laird's father had the records completely put in shape about 1885. They were reorganized into modern files just before the first war." David accepted his demitasse, sipped and set it aside. "There are gaps in early records, but at this point, whatever isn't there probably no longer exists." Andrew was setting a generously-filled brandy snifter beside the rejected demitasse. The Laird picked it up, warmed it in his hands. "These days we simply accumulate data until there's sufficient for a day's work." He sipped contentedly. "And my secretary comes out for a weekend to bring us up to date." He sipped again. "I think you'll find everything Mrs. Ware needs."

"Oh; yes, I know it's simple. Aunt Agnes was here, she told me where to look."

"Here?" Three pairs of eyes stared at me silently. "When was this?" Sholto asked casually . . . but I was instinctively cautious.

"Some time after the first war . . . she and Uncle Fred were invited by the old Laird for the grouse shoot, and she browsed in the records." I shrugged, finishing my coffee. "Would it be *very* rude if I asked to be excused for bed?" I asked Annis. "It really was a long drive, and you know how warm food swiftly overtakes you?" I smiled at David and Sholto sadly. "May I say good night before I fall flat on my nose and disgrace myself forever?"

"Of course, of course! Sleep well! Andrew, see Miss Lennox to her room, will you? Good night, good night . . . see you tomorrow."

The hand soap was lemon verbena, and the bed looked comfortable. My windows framed a clear view of the tower Sholto had called a fortalice. I would look it up as soon as I found a dictionary. There was no doubt it was some sort of watchtower. The night was crystal clear, unbelievably spangled with stars around a moon halfway to the full. In the faint starlight, the fortalice was mysterious, yet not so much a forbidding and unfriendly place as a reassuring guardian. I'd no idea how old it was. History was never my best subject because of dates. My mind goes blank at once when numbers are mentioned. I know there's a significance about 1066, 1649, 1588—but do not ask me what it is.

I could visualize kilted guards keeping watch from the tower with flaming torches. Didn't they used to signal from hill to hill like our Indians . . . or was that the Congo drums?

Leaving only a reading light on behind me, I began to get a perspective of Strathmuir: a sprawling, roughly U-shaped building. I was on the more-or-less straight bottom of the U, with a right-angle wing extending to my left in a series of lighted windows: the Laird's wing.

42

Leaning drowsily against the embrasure I thought it must be a magnificent suite . . . with an immense master chamber at the end, a dressing room, bath for both Laird and Lady. . . .

The lights flicked off, beginning at the center and moving apart, until there were only two windows at either end of the original row. I snapped awake to observe a reduced glow from the inner windows of the Laird's chamber: reading light.

So the Laird no longer slept with his Lady? *He stole her to help him make a good impression, she loves only her own comfort. . . .* Two daughters only—was Annis already past the possibility of an heir? Abandoned, cast aside for failure to provide a son?

I was about to turn away from the chill window when a flickering lantern, swinging vigorously, emerged from around the end of the Laird's wing of Strathmuir. I heard a soft commanding whistle. "Here, lass, come awa' home then," Sholto's voice said. "Where are ye?" He raised the lantern, waved it, whistling again—and from far up the hill leading to the fortalice, I saw a huge collie hurriedly trotting downward. Sholto apparently saw her too, for he stood still until she panted up to him.

"And what were ye doing out this time o'night?" he demanded severely, while she nuzzled affectionately at his free hand. "Och, Jennie, ye're a wild one! Time enough to be looking for Wullie again when your pups are born; he's no use to ye now!" The deep voice was a rich chuckle as Sholto patted the dog's head. They started forward along a path apparently leading directly to the farther wing. In the lantern light, the gay plaid of his kilt swung easily with his stride, while the

43

collie paced docilely beside him.

I stood motionless, observing the harmonious rightness of the man in his natural habitat. Not the Laird's fault he was born in Liverpool—but if he lived to be a hundred, he'd never acquire the gait of Sholto Comyn. In David the Sassenach blood of the chambermaid was evidently stronger than the Gordon of his father. But even George Kirby wasn't pure Scot, I remember.

My eyes followed the striding figure moving along a hillside path, and unconsciously I leaned farther and farther into the corner of the window to watch the man with his dog. Jennie barked sharply, and the lantern swung high as a firm hand restrained her from plunging after some small night animal making for cover. "Shshsh, lass . . ."

The descending arc of the lantern flashed across my window and caught me full face, peering through the draperies. His arm paused so definitely I knew he'd seen me. I prayed he couldn't see me blush at being still awake when I'd long since said I was tired and should have been abed. But he only gestured briefly with the iron-bound lantern. The flickering light softened the rugged planes of his face, illumined the smile. "Good night again, cousin!"

Limply I waved and nodded, watched him retreating with his dog, to vanish around the end of the other wing. I straightened the draperies slowly, wondering. . . .

What was a jilted sweetheart doing here, with his own rooms, managing the estate, an integral part of the Strathmuir household? Sleepy as I was, I came awake at the implications—and instantly discarded them. The man who'd go out at midnight to search for his pregnant collie bitch was not one to be part of a triangle.

Still, just as I fell asleep a clear question flashed through my mind. Why did they wish I had not come?

In daylight I found my way to the main floor more by the scent of bacon than by knowledge. The dining room was deserted, but a long Jacobean side table held a most impressive equipage: eight covered silver dishes over Sterno-type flames! Quietly, I inspected them. There were: Scrambled eggs, sausages, kippers, bacon, oat cakes, lamb kidneys, and creamed *something* that was either flaked fish or chicken. There were two thermos pitchers: orange juice and grape, by the smell. A removable padded igloo covered a tea pot. A huge silver urn containing coffee was accompanied by a smug pitcher of thick cream. At the end, stood a modern toaster, a pile of bread slices and what remained of a pound of butter on an oblong dish.

The dining table held a Lazy Susan, sporting six pots of jams, more cream, a sugar bowl, another half-pound of butter; a small carafe of ice water stood beside a glass, in deference to the American fondness for cold water.

The sight of so much food was almost revolting. Presumably David and Sholto had already break-fasted; they hadn't made a dent in what waited for Annis and me. What became of leftovers? Did the staff get them next morning, or did they go into the swill? If so, the Huntly pigs must make mighty tasty eating.

It was another tiny revelation. I remembered hearing

once that anyone who was starved in childhood never gets over it. Pathetic, that the Laird should have been so very hungry as to need this sort of reassurance.

By American standards, the coffee was vile. I managed a half a cup to wash down a slice of toast. The jam was superb, thick blackberry with no additives. I had another slice to try the gooseberry, which was equally delicious. I wondered where Annis got them. A full assortment would be exactly the present to please Aunt Agnes.

I finished the last bite, lit a cigarette and mused. More than ever I wished I'd never come. I didn't like these people, and they didn't like me. Could I finish in the records today, take a few pictures of house and grounds tomorrow, and be gracefully away before lunch? Every instinct said, *get out before you put your foot into something!*

The serving door swung open and Andrew emerged. He stopped, faintly flustered at sight of me. "Good morning, miss . . . you should have rung for me."

"No need, thank you, Andrew. I found all I wanted."

He eyed my rejected coffee sharply. "You didna like it?"

"Well, no, I'm afraid Americans are fussy about coffee."

He nodded. "Mrs. Frame will make it fresh, the way ye'll tell her."

"No, don't bother her, please. I've had all I want."

"Nay," he insisted, firmly pressing the bell, "she'll be glad to get the hang of it, now she has the chance from a real American."

I sat still, sternly suppressing giggles. How Scottish can you be, to make use of the first American guest to explain the art of coffee-making? I wasn't so sure Mrs. Frame would be happy to know her coffee was undrinkable, but I was wrong. She was delighted. "I think it's the machine, miss. I've the percolator for dinner coffee, but this urn—it defeats me, miss, that it does!"

"It'd defeat anyone but a cafeteria worker," I said. She looked at me questioningly. "It's far too big," I explained, "and I suspect it makes excellent coffee for the full amount, but you probably use only half."

"Did I not tell ye?" Andrew demanded triumphantly.

Mrs. Frame fixed him with a defiant glance. "And what would I do with an entire urn of coffee, Andrew?"

"Make coffee gelatins, or use it to baste the mutton," I suggested.

She eyed me carefully. "Ye'll not be serious, mistress?"

"Entirely," I assured her. "In the States, we use strong coffee for lamb and beef pot roast; in Sweden, they add cream and sugar to the strong coffee. Either way is delicious." I could see her absorbing this thoughtfully. "For breakfast coffee use the percolator; measure half as much coffee as for dinner, that's all." I stood up with a smile. "By the way, where do you get the delicious jams? I'd like to buy some for my aunt."

"Jams?" she echoed. "They're made here. Lady Annis is verra traditional in preserving the crops. I've bottled the raspberries—next week there's blackberries and apricots, then blueberries. Steenie says it's a fine year for them."

Well, well! "When do you smoke the hams and bacons?"

"First week of October," she said absently. "What

47

coffee machine do you use, mistress?"

"Personally, I prefer a Chemex; other people have other tastes."

She nodded. "Andrew, ye'll get me one," she stated, "and Miss Lennox, ye'll instruct me. And if ye'll want preserve for your aunt, there's more than enough. We've not used all of 1962 as yet. I'll put up a box for ye."

Good God, they were *three years* behind? Now I understood the faint resignation in her tone when she said Steenie predicted a bumper crop of blueberries! I could imagine the Laird visiting the pantry stocked with more than could ever be used, and taking comfort in the proof he'd never go hungry again.

Going toward the record room, I wondered cynically whether he'd forbid preserves for Aunt Agnes—and decided he wouldn't. Now that he'd learned about her wealth, he'd part with almost anything in order to please her.

If only I hadn't been lured by Sholto into making a good story the night before! Aunt Agnes was as shrewd as she could be when it came to people. She wouldn't be unstrung to discover the Laird was a money-grubber, for all her Clan reverence. Nor would she censure me for rising to the lure, but I censured myself severely. From that moment on, I was determined to say nothing more. If the Laird knew she'd met his mother, he'd think he was in like Flynn!

Damn Sholto for leading me on—or was it deliberate? For all his contempt of my errand, he knew I was descended from Bettrys. So was Aunt Agnes. I had a sudden certainty that Sholto Comyn was perfectly acquainted with the wealth of Agnes Seton Ware, and had led me to verify this because . . .

Now it made a picture: Sholto, the man to manage land . . . and David, the townsman to handle business. Annis didn't figure in it at all. She'd jilted Sholto for the Laird. But men are capable of discarding emotions in favor of cooperation for ultimate ends. It was worth thinking about. . . .

"Good morning, good morning, Sable. You slept well?" The Laird got up from his desk and came forward, still nervous, ingratiating, shaking hands damply. "Andrew gave you whatever you fancied for breakfast?" In daylight, he was even more rat-faced and pallid, but evidently anxious to be a welcoming host.

"Everything was delicious, aside from the coffee. I hope you won't mind, David," I said, "but in return for real American instructions on coffee, Mrs. Frame offered to send an assortment of Strathmuir jams to Aunt Agnes, who will *adore* them."

To my amazement, after a single blink, David laughed heartily. "*Mind?* My dear Sable, if you can help Mrs. Frame produce a decent cup of coffee, Mrs. Ware may have the entire contents of the storeroom! We'll never use it all, but nothing will persuade Annis to discard her mother's preserving calendar—or that coffee urn. It belonged to her family, and she's still thinking of hunt breakfasts!"

I sensed sardonic contempt in his tone. "Afraid I meddled, David. I told Mrs. Frame to use the percolator for small breakfasts, or buy a Chemex— they aren't very expensive."

"Chemex? I seem to have heard of it." He extended his cigarette case. "Not what you're used to, American blends have more taste—" He flicked his lighter. "But the cost is prohibitive over here. Well, now—first you must sign the register." He led me to a stand, opened a leatherbound book and held out a pen.

I sighed my full name: Sable Ware Gordon-Lennox—and noticed that the last entry was dated 1938: Sir John Compson. The Laird looked at my signature with interest. "Gordon-Lennox?"

"My legal name. We don't use hyphens in America, you know."

"That's so. Well," he slapped the register closed, "where do we begin?"

We? In a library, he finishes first who works alone! "If you'd show me the master file? I know how busy you are, you mustn't let me interfere with your schedule, David."

"No, no, I'll enjoy watching an expert," he said flatteringly and held out a hand. "Do you have a list?"

I thought of the pungent comments in Aunt Agnes's all-too-legible handwriting. "Only shorthand notes," I said swiftly, "but it's only female lines, not much." I headed for the card catalog, looking at him over my shoulder. "One thing—would you mind if I photographed Strathmuir as it is today, to show Aunt Agnes? There'd be a set for you and Annis, of course— although it's only fair to say a number of chichi magazines would pay high for permission to reproduce." I began flipping through card entries. "You might give the money to some local charity. . . ."

"Photograph what you like, Sable—but publicity . . . I doubt Annis would agree," he said nervously.

"I've never allowed photographs of myself, even for business reasons . . . Laird of the Clan, somehow it's not quite . . ."

"They're not needed for this sort of layout," I said, rapidly noting index numbers. "Merely good shots of principal rooms, family treasures, the chair used by Robert Bruce or someone . . . but if Annis wouldn't even like rooms described in the public press, forget it, please?" I smiled at him apologetically. "I really want a few shots for Aunt Agnes. The rest was only an idea to make money for charity at no cost to yourself. Afraid I'm a big American when it comes to figuring all the angles."

"Yes, I knew a number of Americans in the war!" He laughed reflectively. "I learned a lot about *angles!* Take all the pictures you like, my dear," he decided. "Then we'll see, eh?"

"Right!" I shut the file briskly. "Ready to go!"

The Laird's eyes narrowed. "How quickly you did it! Now what are you needing?" He held out his hand and this time I gave him the numbered list. "The oldest manuscripts are in locked cabinets—all photographed or copied before my time." His eyes were flicking over my numbers. "I put in a temperature control to preserve originals, so unless you must have them, I'd rather not open those files. The antiquarian people said air was dangerous."

"Quite right. I need nothing before 1860."

"Good, good!" He returned the list. "I'll leave you to it then. The catalog begins here for the shelves, and here for single papers."

The Laird went back to his desk, and I moved along searching for my references. In five minutes I had two old diaries and was settled at a corner table. I wasn't pleased to be under the Laird's surveillance—there was no doubt he was keeping an eye on me, despite his apparent preoccupation with papers and occasional phone calls.

The instant I'd finished the first diaries (getting six of Aunt Agnes's dates) and rose to replace them, David was there asking alertly, "Can I help?"

"I'm only getting the next numbers on the list, thanks. Here they are." Settling to work again, I smiled at his eagerness to assist Aunt Agnes's niece. What little angle was the Laird cooking up? I found two more dates and should have put away that diary, but I was caught by the scurrilous wit of the writer. I'd never thought Victorian ladies more than surface Simon Pure; here was the proof that at least one spinster knew more of La Dolce Vita, even if by hearsay, than I did. On and on I read, until David said, "Lunchtime!"

My watch said one-thirty, and my tummy agreed. I picked up the diary, meaning to ask if I might take it with me. "I usually have a tray," he said. "Will you join me, or would you rather have a proper meal at table?" I inspected his tray: cold beef, garden lettuce and potato salad, oat cake, farm butter, Stilton, and a pewter tankard of ale.

"May I eat here, if I'm not in the way?"

"Delighted to have company! Andrew?" The Laird sat back smiling at me. "You're finding what you want?"

"Yes, nearly through—but I'm wasting time," I said, sitting in the desk chair beside him. "Lady Catherine Seton's Diary of about 1870 is irresistible! D'you know the story of the grouse shoot for the Prince of Wales, and how everyone contributed a bird so Victoria wouldn't find out he had been flirting with Lady P and had never left the house? Who *was* Lady P?"

"I've no idea," he confessed. "I'm not too keen on this sort of thing, Sable. I expect you know I came in sideways? Well, I wasn't prepared for any of it. My mother was a servant, my father was dead. I got a board school education, no more. I drove a truck for a while, then I was in the Army." His fingers played with a paper clip on the tooled leather-bound blotter. "When I came home, Mother was dead and I was Laird," he finished. "I'd all to learn and no one to help me. It was a problem."

Reluctantly I was impressed by the simplicity of his words. "A problem you certainly solved," I said, "and you had Annis to help."

His fingers twisted the paper clip, tossed it aside. "Yes, I had Annis," he agreed. The door opened and Andrew rolled a tea cart forward. Andrew rapidly set forth my lunch on the edge of the desk. "Ye'll fancy the ale, mistress?" he asked anxiously. "There's lemonade or tea . . . ?"

"I'll try the ale, thank you, Andrew."

David picked up his fork and eyed me shrewdly as the butler disappeared. "D'you really like ale," he remarked, "or are you merely being a good guest?"

"Six of one, half dozen of t'other," I said, attacking the beef. "I'm not wild about ale, but it seems more correct, sort of Pickwickian." I munched vigorously, took a swallow of ale. It was amazingly smooth. "Mmmm. Despite the impassioned pleas of Madison Avenue for *brisk* Lipton Tea, Americans—if they drink tea at all—like it as weak as you people make coffee."

David chuckled. "With lemon, as I remember."

"Occasionally we decorate the lemon slices with whole cloves," I nodded, sampling the potato salad. It was perfect. "You have a good cook, David!"

"Only Mrs. Frame. She was with Mrs. Richmond until her death. Annis persuaded her to return to us. She has all the family recipes. However," David confided, "I'll admit I detest haggis."

"Don't apologize. Aunt Agnes can't stand it either. She says it's worse than *boudin,* but better than scrapple," I snorted. "You haven't lived till you've rejected Philadelphia scrapple, David!"

He frowned faintly, dissecting the Stilton. "Some sort of tasteless fried mush with ground pork entrails," he grimaced, "and they put maple syrup on it and eat it for breakfast?"

"That's it."

He transferred a wedge of cheese to my plate and took one for himself. "If the English government had ever eaten scrapple, they'd have taken the Colonial Rebellion seriously," he said. "Any people who could eat *that* for breakfast must be indomitable."

I was beginning to like the Laird better, now that we were alone and informal. "We also have apple butter, chitterlings, and rattlesnake steaks," I advised. "You're right, we are indomitable."

"Not only do we have haggis, we have winkles," he returned snootily. We were sitting there laughing like fools, wiping our eyes on our napkins, when the door swung open and Sholto stared in at us. "Come in, come in," David beckoned.

"Sorry to interrupt," Sholto said after a moment. "I

54

wanted figures on Eylesbury. I thought you were gone to Liverpool for a board meeting."

"I put it off till Friday." The Laird tossed his napkin across the tray. "Have you eaten? Andrew'll bring a tray."

"Thanks, no—I lunched with Annis. She didn't know you were here either." Sholto crossed to a shelf, drawing out a ledger, setting it on the long table, bending over, turning pages, making notes . . . ignoring us completely.

So completely that I knew there was something about finding me laughing uproariously with the Laird that had put Lord Aboyne in a furious mood.

David was unconcerned. "You've done enough, you need fresh air!" He stood up and held out his hand. "Come, let's start the pictures. What sort of camera do you use, Sable?"

"Nikon-F, 35mm, various lenses," I said automatically. "I've two: one black-and-white, one color. . . ." In the doorway, as David gallantly opened the door, I glanced back and met Sholto's eyes, glaring at me, dark with anger.

Even though I'd never seen it before, I recognized *murder* in those eyes before he swung away and bent over the table once more. . . .

Chapter 4

Why?

Changing into walking slacks, checking the cameras and sliding extra film into my jacket pockets, I wondered confusedly why the Earl of Aboyne and Sutherland should so loathe me? Should I have lunched with Annis, instead of having a tray alone with the Laird? Probably, by European standards. I'd forgotten the conventions for an unmarried woman. In a way I'd never known them, couldn't quite believe anyone still took them seriously . . . for why should there be anything questionable about eating alone with a man who'd been alone with me for hours over the files?

I looked uncertainly at the remaining dates on Aunt Agnes's list—so few to get, if only I'd finished before photographing . . . but there was no way to refuse the Laird's offer. Oh well, reverse everything: photograph today, finish the dates tomorrow—and I could still leave before lunch. I slung the cameras about my neck, found my way to the stairs, and trotted down to find the Laird leaning on a blackthorn stick, attired in a rough tweed jacket and a deerstalker hat. "Sherlock Holmes!" I said admiringly. "Are we looking for the speckled band or the hound of the Baskervilles?"

He swung around at my voice and smiled. Somehow, when he wasn't trying to be anything but just himself, David Kirby-Gordon wasn't half-bad. No Adonis, but not unattractive in a ferrety sort of way—and extremely quick for whatever he did know, even if he'd had scant schooling. He eyed my hair with a grin. "Surely we're the Red-Headed League?" In a split second he'd understood me."

"Couldn't I be the Study in Scarlet?"

"My dear Sable, I've no doubt you can and will be anything you choose!" With a laugh, he caught my elbow and turned me to the door. "You're one of the nicest things I've met in twenty years. I can't say how glad I am that you came, Sable."

"But you weren't at first, were you?" I said involuntarily, following him up a path apparently leading to the tower. "You rather wished I hadn't asked to use the family records, didn't you, David? I'd have understood if you'd refused."

"Did you think I would?"

"In a way. But I'm glad you didn't. Even if you didn't know Aunt Agnes was elderly, it was pleasant of you to do her a kindness," I said, a bit breathlessly. "I must write her I'm here."

"Leave your letters on the hall table. Andrew sends the post bag to catch the six o'clock mail train." David turned, smiling. "Going too fast for you? Take a breather, eh? You'll get an idea of the estate."

Automatically, I unslung my cameras. The light was

perfect; it was unnecessary to bracket exposures. These would all be good, with more color than I'd realized: climbing roses hugging the gray stone wings, a formal flower garden guarded by topiaries at the corners, and a carpet of heather spreading randomly upward. David leaned on his stick, smoking silently while I murmured enthusiastically. "Wonderful color! I suppose the garden is Annis's pride and joy?"

"Only vegetables," he said absently. I must have looked surprised because he smiled faintly. "She had to handle the Rhynie garden during the war when Mr. Richmond had a stroke. Poor girl, she knew nothing, lost practically all the crops the first year. They'd have starved except for the old Laird; he kept them going while Annis took a course. Now she supervises the kitchen garden; Sholto handles livestock and field crops . . ." David carefully ground out his cigarette and straightened up. ". . . and they both produce far too much," he ended drily. "Are you rested? Shall we go on, Sable?"

"Yes, please. I'm dying to see the view from the tower." Tactfully, I abandoned Annis and overproduction. "Sholto called it a fortalice, but I don't know what that is."

"Forerunner of a fortress," the Laird said. "Simply a tower on high ground, as you see. Usually there were several, roughly placed at the corners of a demesne, with guards signalling each other at night . . . not only against human enemies but against wolves or mountain lions marauding in the flocks. Later, in feudal times, they built the towers closer together and connected them with walls. That's a fortress. Or if it was a walled town, it was called a fort."

I wondered what encyclopedia he'd digested to provide that précis. "Are there other fortalices around Huntly, then?"

"Originally this was one of a string leading over the hills, to connect with the towers for Inverness." He was still speaking by rote. "They were built by the Comyns, I forget the dates, and they were nearly all destroyed in the 16th—or was it the 15th Century?" David shook his head. "Ask Sholto, he knows. . . ."

I wouldn't have asked Lord Aboyne the time of day, after that final glance! "So this is all that's left?"

"Yes, and in very bad shape. We don't permit visitors now. I'm not sure we can get to the top any longer, Sable. Last time I was here there were fallen stair blocks. The view is exceptional but not worth a broken leg," he said, hauling me up the final yard of rocky path. His arm was surprisingly vigorous. "Now, rumble about while I have a look inside. You'll get a number of good shots."

I'd finished both rolls and reloaded before he came back. "I think we can try for the top, but take nothing you don't absolutely need, Sable." He looked worriedly at the cameras swaying from my shoulders. "Is there any way to keep the camera still? I want your hands free. Have nothing that might tangle your knees or feet."

"Tie them together with my scarf." Eventually they were securely anchored to the rear of my belt, and I stepped into the fortalice. I could see why David was dubious. It was a roughly circular, stone-floored chamber with the remains of a fireplace, its chimney only a gaping hole where stones had fallen away. The staircase, a spiral of stones, was crumbling at the outer edge and lacking any sort of handrail. There were two gaps, one above the chimney hole, another on the final turn to the top.

I ascended slowly, following the steps up and up to an opening with sky above. It looked as far away as the top of the Empire State Building, and I was frankly petrified. I'd never been conscious of height-phobia, and undoubtedly I could get up—but would I ever get down, I wondered with a gulp. The Laird went up the first few steps, saying, "I went to the top before. It's quite secure—but keep close to the wall." I expected my face showed terror because he stopped. "Are you sure you want to try, Sable? Don't mind saying if it makes you nervous—Annis can't even look at it."

She couldn't, eh? "Well, I may have to crawl down backwards, David, but I don't mind if you won't." It wasn't too bad after all. The steps were shallow; I didn't even need David's hand to step across the gaps. When I finally came out onto the lookout, I wouldn't have missed it for the world—even if they had to rig a breeches buoy to hoist me down afterwards!

Fields, hills, a flash of water through trees—Strathmuir itself, nestled under the protection of the fortaliee, with stone wings flung out like motherly arms about gardens and barns . . . privet-edged paths leading to byres and sties . . . chicken coops discreetly hidden behind a knoll. David untied my equipment and leaned against the parapet. I took picture after picture until both rolls were finished once more and I'd refilled. "Can I get more film in Strathbogie, David, or should I save some?"

"No, there's a good photographic supply store in the Square."

Cows in the farthest fields, lambs closer to home . . . a magnificent stand of trees in the distance. But the light was changing now and I couldn't chance failure. I'd probably never get up here again. I leaned to the light, checking settings. There was a row of stone projections beneath the crenels. "What are those?"

"Bracing stones for the beams supporting the roof."

"Oh." I was positioned for a final shot of Strathmuir that was already The House of the Golden Windows in the shower of sunlight. In the rear finder, a flurry of wings . . . pigeons startled by motion, and a man and dog rounding the edge of the barn: Sholto and his Jennie.

Abruptly I went across to the opposite side. There the land was higher, then levelled off and swept down over more fields to a small stone building. "What's that?"

"The mill on the Deveron."

"Do you still use it?"

"Yes. It's leased, but on condition that we can operate the mill each harvest. More tradition than profit," David said. "We do our own flour, and the Huntly mill is open to anyone who fancies stone-ground grains. There are a few old-time millers, a few youngsters being trained. Annis thought it silly to repair for three months a year." The Laird absently lit cigarettes, handed me one. "There's not much future here for young people. This gives them a few months steady wages before winter, an incentive to stay on the land. Sholto thought it a good idea."

"Of course, but couldn't it be full time? In America, stone-ground grains are a high-priced gourmet item. The snob-appeal of Huntly should be immense. I suppose," I murmured uneasily, "it's only another American 'angle'."

"One I've often considered." He drew a long breath. "I'll put it bluntly: until last night I thought Mrs. Ware was merely another distant relative claiming kinship for her own prestige. The letters I get from all over the world," he snorted, "from people who don't even know the Laird's name! Well, now that I know Mrs. Ware is seriously interested in the Clan, she could help me if she would. Would it be wrong to ask her help?"

I'd known this was coming, and I had the answer. "I'll give you the name and address of her business managers. You must write them, setting forth your proposition exactly as for a bank loan. It's a family rule to express no opinion, you understand? So the only help I can give you is: *don't* write to her, David. She'll turn it over to the business people—and no matter how sound your proposal, you'll have one strike against you for having approached her directly."

"I see," David narrowed his eyes thoughtfully. "I'm not trying to take advantage of a rich old woman, Sable. I need a bit of venture capital. I could probably get it from a bank, but I'd rather not stretch myself too thin . . . or I might sink the ship for a ha'porth of tar. What you don't know is that when I became Laird I found *nothing*." David's thin lips tightened bitterly. "Twenty years ago there was Strathmuir and *land* . . . lots of land, to a city slum kid. There were corporate interests . . . I'd never seen a stock certificate. The old Laird was old. His last years he let things slip. It didn't matter—everyone protected him. Because he was *born* the Laird.

"I was different—fair game, a Sassenach outlander. I

was lucky, at that. People were honest out of respect for the title, or I'd have been bankrupt. But for me personally, it was the letter of the law and explain nothing," he said evenly. "I wasn't born a gentleman and I made constant mistakes. But there's one thing about a Liverpool water rat—you learn early on to fight for survival. It didn't take long before I was ready to fight for the Laird's rights, even if no one wanted me to enjoy them."

He was getting through to me. Aunt Agnes had said, "Remember he's not a gentleman," and the Laird's sister Margaret hadn't liked him—but they were an older, more formal generation. I could well imagine the unspoken dislike that greeted a sharp-faced kid twenty years back. But a glance at the estate and the comfortable house showed that David Kirby-Gordon had what it took—which was probably a hell of a lot of guts and sweat. Doubly hard for an uneducated man, and more power to him! And I told him so.

"You must be very proud, and rightly, at everything you've done to stabilize and increase your heritage, David."

"Am I?" he murmured sardonically. "Yes, I suppose I am, although it wasn't done willingly. I had no choice—but yes, I even surprised myself." He laughed softly. "Sometimes, when I'm sitting at a long polished mahogany company board table and telling a dozen dignified gentlemen who went to Harrow, Eton, Oxford, Cambridge, what to do," David grinned disarmingly, "I'll admit I do feel a bit proud of myself, Sable.

"I've done well with the business. I did even better when I persuaded Sholto to manage the land. I won't explain the arrangement, but it's advantageous for both of us." He stopped abruptly, eyeing me. "I've told you more than I ever admitted to anyone. You're—far too easy to talk to, Sable," he remarked, half-annoyed. "American women always are, for some reason."

"Because we're so smart," I returned. "When *we* listen, a man knows he's understood—and I think I understand which way you're headed, David."

"Do you? Tell me. . . ."

I moved absently along the parapet. "You've concentrated—wisely, I'm sure—on building the capital investments," I said slowly. "Now you're ready to build prestige for the state: Huntly Mill flours, Strathmuir jams, Gordon bacon, ham and sausage, perhaps a frozen vegetable line." I was looking at the overproductive kitchen garden. "For this you will need everything: freezers, efficient packaging, advertising, salesmen, distribution—the works, as we say in America. But you're not sure you're justified in mortgaging Clan capital for a totally unfamiliar enterprise. So what you want to know now is: will your rich American kinswoman lend at low interest?"

There was a long pause, while his gray eyes flickered. Then he said, "Yes! Lord, you're clever, Sable! Do you think Mrs. Ware might agree?"

"If you convince her business advisers it's a sound proposal, I suspect Aunt Agnes will lend without interest," I nodded calmly. "It's exactly the project to catch her fancy, David—but it has to be businesslike!"

He swung around, gently pounding fist to palm and walking back and forth. "I hadn't meant to try for another few years, but if you think she might . . ." he muttered, half to himself. "Freezers would be simplest for a trial, but there's the distribution. Our smokehouse produces only a bit more than we normally use ourselves. Sholto offered his, at Aboyne and Comynhaugh, but there'd still not be enough for a marketing operation. We'd make ends meet for small local sales. I thought maybe we might start with what we have, but I doubt we'd reach far enough to build any demand."

I hadn't liked him last night and I was still wary, but more receptive. He wasn't my type of man but I sensed exectuive ability. I'd a hunch if David Kirby-Gordon started anything, he'd work eighteen hours a day to put it over. "I can't *say* anything to Aunt Agnes," I said impulsively. "However, I can report this conversation in my diary."

"Diary?"

"We agreed that I'd send occasional postcards and that I'd keep a daily diary for her to read when I get home. If your timing is right, by the time her business managers arrive with the current investment suggestions, she will have read this interchange. Get it?"

David's eyes narrowed sharply. "It will probably take six weeks to prepare facts and figures," he said, looking into space. "Perhaps eight weeks might be better, to be certain nothing is overlooked. That should do it, don't you think?" At my nod, he grinned. "Sable—whether or not, I thank you from the bottom of my heart!" He slid a bony arm about me, hugged me convulsively, kissed my temple and let me go. As David moved aside I found I was staring at Sholto's dark blue eyes.

Jennie sprang forward with a joyous bark. "Hello, old girl," David patted her head absently. "Sholto?"

"Yes?"

"Oh, you're there, are you? Come and tell Sable the history of the fortalice, will you?" The Laird moved to the other end of the lookout, Jennie trotting beside him. After a minute's pause, Sholto came toward me.

"It was built in the twelfth century by William Comyn; in the fourteenth century it passed to a girl, Matilda, who married George Gordon," he said. "His sister married a Seton, his son was the first Earl of Huntly, his grandson the first Marquess . . . the fourth Marquess was created Duke of Gordon, the fifth Duke died without issue, the marquessate went to his cousin, who was the fifth Earl of Aboyne . . ." Sholto's voice was toneless, as though reading a guidebook, and he was still stepping toward me. . . .

Instinctively, I retreated a pace at a time before the cold fury in his eyes. I half-thought he meant to—oh, I don't know what: slap me, choke me, hurt me physically. . . . I stared wildly over his shoulder, but David's back was turned; he'd completely forgotten me. Sholto was saying, "The sister of the fifth Duke married a Lennox who was fourth Duke of Richmond . . . the sixth Earl of Aboyne married a sister of the ninth Earl of Sutherland who was a Countess in her own right . . . the Gordons of Gight were ancestors of Lord Byron, and the American Gordons stem from Alexander Gordon who was a tutor in South Carolina . . ."

I was trembling . . . he'd got me backed against the farthest merlon. And David was lost in the clouds of masculine figuring a good thirty feet away. Even if I screamed, would he hear me in his concentration on the proposal for Aunt Agnes? And if he did, what was I to say? "Please, *please*," I whispered, anguished, "I

67

haven't done anything, Sholto. Why d'you hate me?"

He stepped back a pace, raising his chin arrogantly. "What are you doing here, cousin? You came to get some dates for a rich aunt," he said, deadly soft. "Why don't you get them and leave, instead of courting danger among the ruins?"

I stared at him dumbly, until he turned away and went to stand beside David. They leaned over the crenel, talking quietly, while Sholto pointed here or there. Evidently estate business. I sagged against my side of the parapet, struggling to prevent tears, taking deep, even, deliberate breaths to control inner shakes. I was conscious of a bewilderment that was very nearly terror. I'd met people who didn't much like me; Annis was one, and the emotion was mutual. But this was the first time I'd ever encountered pure hatred. What had I done? Or was that his reaction to any intruder? He'd disliked me at sight, I remembered . . . only softened a bit when I mentioned the Campbells.

I couldn't think then, the men were coming toward me. Oh, *God,* we were about to go down those crumbling stairs! I swallowed hard. It was no good. On top of the scene with Sholto, I knew I wasn't going to be able to do it. I wouldn't have minded crawling down backwards with David alone; I might even have tried going forward. If only they'd go first . . . but they'd simply wait for me politely at the bottom.

"I'd lost track of time! Go along, Jennie," David lightly whacked the collie's rump and she lumbered heavily but sure-footed ahead of us. "Now, Sable, are you going to be able to get down safely? Suppose I go first and you put your hands on my shoulders, not looking at anything? Shall we tie the camera together?

68

You have everything? Sholto, perhaps you can steady her from the rear. . . ." The Laird fussed about, while Sholto eyed me impassively.

"Our cousin is uneasy with heights?" He thrust my gear at David. "You start down, I'll bring her." Casually, he turned and swung me into his arms. "Put your arms around my neck, cousin; the balance will be more comfortable."

It was the ultimate humiliation, but I had no choice. One glimpse of David simply disappearing down the opening . . . ugh . . . I put my arms about Sholto and closed my eyes—which only made me aware of shaving cologne, softly smoky tweed, a whiff of fresh lavender, plus strong arms and cheek resting lightly against my temple.

I was apparently no burden at all. Sholto merely walked down the fortalice stairs, stepping easily across the missing stones, while I clung to him, unable to suppress a dry sob of ignominy. "Shhh, lass, we're nearly down, I have ye safe." His deep voice was a replica of his tone to Jennie, but I relaxed until we were standing still. When I raised my head, I was looking straight into his blue eyes.

Sholto made no effort to put me down. Amazingly, all his fury had vanished. "Now, you're not to do this again, cousin," he said, giving me a little shake. "Take your snapshots, by all means, but you'll go nowhere outside house and home gardens without my permission, understand?"

"Yes, but didn't . . . I mean, David was with me." I hadn't enough fight even to protest his contemptuous "snapshots."

Sholto sighed, faintly exasperated. "But *I'm* the

estate agent, Sable. Even the Laird doesn't know where we've vermin traps because he's no man for walking. Ye silly little clunch!" he said, half-affectionately. "Och, *dhu,* when I saw ye aloft!" He exhaled deeply and grinned. "I'm thankful to have got ye down in one piece, lass. And I'm not minded to find ye caught with a broken ankle in a polecat trap!"

He set me on my feet, straightened my jacket and chucked me casually under the chin, like an elderly uncle to a small child. "That's an order!" he said briskly, turning me to face the house and lightly slapping my fanny. "Go along with ye."

I went.

Far ahead, the Laird, carrying the cameras, walked swiftly across the garden to a rear door. I scurried after him as quickly as possible . . . I'd tell him, I'd ask him why, I'd leave at once, I wouldn't stay a moment where I wasn't wanted. . . . "David, David, wait!" He didn't hear me. When I raced breathlessly across the garden and opened the door, he was gone.

Within was only an empty corridor. And on the fortalice path behind me, hands on hips, was the motionless, implacable figure of Sholto, making certain of my obedience. . . .

Chapter 5

The travel-clock said quarter to four, and Andrew was carefully placing my cameras on the chaise longue. He eyed my slacks and cleared his throat. "Tea is at four-thirty in the solarium. Ye'll have ample time to change your clothes," he said tactfully. "Is there anything I can do for ye, Miss Lennox?"

"Have my car brought around, please?"

He was startled, but too well trained to ask questions. "Certainly, miss."

I'd had time for sober second thoughts. It was not possible to complain, make scenes, flounce away in a huff—that would have suited Sholto perfectly! I'd been legitimately invited by the Laird, who might have had an axe to grind but was still a friendly host. Damned if I'd be chased away by the estate agent. "I need more film, Andrew. The Laird says there's a shop."

"Aye, MacDanald's in the Square," Andrew said. "Ye'll say ye're from Strathmuir, mistress, so Ranald'll serve ye himself."

As I exchanged slacks for a skirt, ran a comb

through my hair and powdered my nose, I giggled inwardly: what sort of film would I be sold if I were *not* from Strathmuir? Swiftly I packed the finished rolls, which were addressed to the London processor, and on impulse bundled the day's notes into my handbag. I'd get a large envelope in the town and send them to Aunt Agnes. Even if she couldn't decipher the shorthand, she'd have fun playing with the dates until I got back to transcribe.

I found a sheet of crested notepaper. "Here's part— the place is lovely, the people are peculiar, will finish tomorrow and go back to Campbells, love, Sable."

Andrew was hovering when I came downstairs. "I won't be more than an hour—and if Lady Annis is surprised, perhaps you could hint that Americans don't take tea very seriously."

His lips twitched faintly. "Aye. Ye'll find your way alone?"

"Yes, thanks, Andrew."

It was much easier coming down from Strathmuir than climbing up to it. Within fifteen minutes I was parking in front of MacDanald's. The Strathbogie post office was only three doors away.

Andrew was right. The instant I told a pimply assistant I was from Strathmuir there was a subterranean muttering, and A Very Superior Personage issued forth majestically from the rear. Ranald MacDanald had everything, knew his business thoroughly and after a slight chat tacitly accepted that I knew it as well. He cautiously agreed that my color processor was "verra good—I'll no say the best, but trustwairthy." Then, he professionally repacked my rolls and stepped along to the post, "the way ye'll be certain of correct handling, mistress."

By the time we'd parted, he'd given me a wealth of sound information on exposures, correct angles, best local views. He was still a Scot, so it was not something for nothing! Ranald dearly wanted a copy of the shots I considered best—for window display. "That way people'll see for themselves color film is worth the expense."

Driving back to Strathmuir, I thought this was a land, a people, I could live among happily. Their absurdities were so logical, their integrity so literal. From top to bottom, they were alike, from Lord Everard and Lady Jean to Ranald MacDanald and Andrew. I felt amazingly at home—except for David, Annis and Sholto. That was food for thought in itself. Why should the only lack of rapport arise in the one place a Gordon kinswoman should feel most at ease? Aunt Agnes had expected difficulties because the Laird was not a gentleman. Ironic that the only problem stemmed from the man who was. . . .

It was close to five when I drove into the cobbled courtyard. Andrew was already hastening down the steps for my packages. "I'll put them in your room. Sandy'll berth the car. Ye'll want to wash your hands— this way, Miss Lennox." All of which I gathered meant that it was the unforgivable sin to be tardy for food. Poor Annis.

She was definitely pinch-lipped when I came into the summer salon. "Yes, of course, Sable—although it wasn't at all necessary to go in person. A note of what you wanted, and Sandy would have got it when he went to the post. Now I'm afraid we must have fresh tea," she said resignedly. "This will be stewed. Andrew?"

"If it's not too much trouble I'll have some of this with a glass of ice," I said. "A pity to waste it."

"Certainly, if you wish." She watched in blank silence while I fixed the tall glass, adding sugar and a squeeze of lemon. "Mmmm, very refreshing."

"Have some of the sandwiches and cake," she said absently, eyeing my glass. "You mean one can use stewed tea for this drink, Sable? Isn't it bitter?"

"It's better freshly made," I conceded, "but this is perfectly drinkable. The ice dilutes the tea, the lemon juice and sugar disguise the flavor." I finished the glass, fixed another, and was suddenly hungry. The sandwiches were watercress and cucumber, very dainty and delicious. I had six; I could have finished the plate, but remembering last night's dinner, I restrained myself.

Annis was lost in thought. Presumably the Strathmuir menu would henceforth feature stewed tea over ice. The Laird was equally absorbed in private reflections, no doubt considering his proposal for Aunt Agnes. It struck me as wickedly funny that we should all silently be concentrating on food, purely because I, who couldn't care less, had upset the balance of power. David was thinking how to make money out of Annis's overproduction, while she was planning to "preserve" stewed tea.

The flick of my lighter roused David. He leaned forward, neatly replacing his teacup on the tray. "You got all you needed at MacDanald's, Sable?"

"Yes, thank you, David. I thought I'd photograph in morning light tomorrow—take perhaps an hour for the rest of Aunt Agnes's dates, and get away about three

74

o'clock tomorrow afternoon."

"Tomorrow?" he echoed. "Nonsense! No, no, I won't hear of it, Sable. You'll never get all the pictures you'd like, and Thursday's the opening of the grouse season. Mrs. Ware will enjoy an account of it." He smiled triumphantly. "I went back through the guest books and she was here in 1928."

Another four days? "Terribly kind of you," I said rapidly, "but I'm sure your list is complete. I'd just be taking space needed for more important people. Besides, the Campbells expect me. . . ."

"Exactly! But we'll be happy to have them here. My dear Sable, you don't understand. The Glorious Twelfth of August is a tradition, something you of all people will appreciate . . . and only a few days off. No, I insist. Annis, tell Sable she's not to think of leaving."

"Of course you must stay, Sable." Annis then looked at David blankly. "But I thought you meant to be in Manchester. Are you not going then?"

"Miss the Glorious Twelfth? My dear Annis, do use your head," he remarked pleasantly. "The Laird traditionally entertains and we've special reason this year: our American cousin. The usual house party, but a little more festive, eh? What a chance for your cameras, Sable!"

Even as I searched wildly for something to say in polite refusal, David was springing to his feet and rubbing his hands together in satisfaction. "Why didn't we think of this before, Annis? I'll write Lord Everard at once—there's just time to catch the post. . . ."

She looked after him in absolute bewilderment, while I was torn between sardonic amusement and fury. *I* was the bait to lure the Lord Lieutenant to Strathmuir! "I can't understand David at all," Annis was murmuring. "For years he's paid no attention . . . Sholto invites a few local people sometimes, but we haven't had the banquet or dance for a long while."

"Does David not handle a gun then?"

"Yes, of course. He's extraordinarily good, but he always said he didn't like First Day—he hates to wait." She was flustered, suddenly on her feet. "Excuse me, Sable. Such short notice, I hadn't planned . . ."

"Couldn't I just leave tomorrow as I planned? I feel I'm upsetting everything, making unnecessary work for you. . . ."

Annis looked at me. "But if David has got the Campbells for the Twelfth, it will be worth any effort," she said with unexpected tartness, and went away before I could say anything.

I finished my iced tea, had another three sandwiches and debated. This was one hell of a predicament. While I could admire the way David had managed his surprise move so smoothly, I resented the status of pawn for his game. Undeniably, I was intrigued by the chance to film a grouse shoot. Why shouldn't I let the Laird gamble a big party for the American cousin? I was just mad enough not to care if the Campbells declined and Aunt Agnes's advisers rejected his proposition.

In a way, I'd no choice but to stay. The Laird had neatly spiked my guns by inviting Lord Everard. Damn clever, Lord David! I thought cynically. All right, he could play his game, and I'd play mine. I'd take my films, I'd enjoy the festivities—and if he had any complaints, I'd lay it on the line: You gambled—and lost.

Going up to my room, I found the silver lining to the situation. Ooooh, wouldn't Sholto be *livid!*

Stripping off clothes, soaking and rinsing vigorously in the shower, I was sinfully happy at the thought of his discomfiture. I came out of the water humming "Johnny One Note," which is the only thing I can sing, and wrapped the bath sheet sarong-fashion. I went to the desk to write up the day's conversation. . . . It was going to take time, but I'd promised the Laird to record fully.

The diary lock was open.

I looked at it blankly. Had I failed to relock last night? Not that the lock was much use; a hairpin, a long fingernail would open it. I locked the diary only to keep the pages pressed straight. I realized that not only was it open, but also it was not where I'd left it. I'd written that note to Aunt Agnes with the fat black-bound book pushed aside.

Now it sat in the center of the blotter.

I shivered slightly in the early night air. I was positive someone had been in my room, had opened the diary, and had inspected the entries.

Nervously, I scanned what I'd written the night before: a comment on the amount of food, descriptions of Annis, Sholto, David, and a report of the conversation that identified *rich* Mrs. Ware. Nothing too pungent, thank heavens! Yet why had anyone wanted to read it? Could I have been mistaken? I snatched up my attaché case. The contents were there, but disarranged. The address book belonged in the first section, the undelivered letters of introduction to people on the Continent belonged in the middle, the potpourri of shopping addresses, *pension* lists and so on was at the back. Everything was now reversed.

Why? Sholto, looking for some way to get rid of me? No, because only David knew about the diary—or had he told Sholto? The estate agent was free to come and go unquestioned, and he would automatically have been told that Miss Lennox was gone to Strathbogie for fresh film. Had he been searching my papers while the Laird was scheming up this party?

Slowly, I discarded the towel, slipped into stockings and fresh underwear, did my face and hair—and tried to be analytical. Sholto had thought David was in Liverpool that day; Annis thought he'd be in Manchester next Thursday. I'd a hunch David never said anything beyond bald statements. So cancelled appointments and sudden plans for a houseparty would seem incomprehensible.

But why inspect my papers? What could anyone expect to find? Dimly, an idea took shape: it wasn't me, or my photographs, or keeping the Laird at Strathmuir —but something in the record room.

No one had worked in the files since David became Laird. Why had I been favored? Pure accident: Annis, innocently answering a letter while he was away. He'd have weaseled out, but the chance to stand well with the Lord Lieutenant had been irresistible. They'd expected a fluttery middle-aged spinster; they'd got a young librarian well-versed with file systems! That must have been a shock, I thought drily. He'd been relieved that I wanted only late Victorian dates. However, he'd still wanted to look at my list—that was what they were looking for, and it had been in my handbag together with the notes. Whatever it was they didn't want me to find, was from an earlier period—because Sholto was in on it, too. He'd done his part by rudeness; what would he say when he found the Laird was risking an extended stay, a party, for the chance to get some of Mrs. Ware's money?

My first impulse was to flatly refuse a party arranged only for ulterior motives, but again, I simmered down. I was still indignant. Wait and see, I decided finally, and scrawled a note to Lord Everard, saying in essence, "Don't come for my sake alone, I'd love the chance to film, but I'm so embarrassed at having it turn into a formal party on my account, I'd almost rather leave. Oh, why didn't you tell me about the Glorious Twelfth!"

There was a tap at the door. "Come in."

Andrew announced, "The Lady Annis is descending."

"Miss Lennox will not be far behind." I sealed the envelope. "Have I missed the post?"

"For tonight, but ye'll give me your letter, the way Sandy'll set it for Geordie Milkman to collect tomorrow morning. Ye'll like it to go special," he stated.

"Do you always mastermind Strathmuir guests, Andrew?"

"Only when they're Gordons. Will there be anything else, miss?"

"Yes," I said, stepping into my evening pumps. "You're a Gordon yourself, are ye not? So ye'll wait five seconds until I've stepped into this blasted dinner dress and ye'll finish pulling up the back zipper, the way I'll not come undressed in the middle o' dinner."

"How did ye know I was a Gordon?" he asked, amazed, facing the door while I slid into the dress.

"The heart knows its own, Andrew. Zipper, please?" He did the final inches in silence. "Thank you, Andrew." I bent to the dressing mirror for a last touch to my hair. In the glass I could see the old man smiling to himself as he opened the door. "'Tis a braw bairn ye are," he murmured, and went away.

I felt warm all over. Andrew's approval was worth more than that of David, Annis and Sholto put together. Sheer guesswork told me he was a clansman. Nothing else explained his care to help me appear at my best in unfamiliar terrain. How much did he know or suspect about his employers? Nothing of the record room, of course. That would be outside his territory. As I went down to the summer salon, I bet myself that Andrew's evaluation of the Laird and Lady Annis would be incredibly accurate. I wondered what he thought of Sholto, Earl of Aboyne and Sutherland.

For that matter, what did *I* think of the Earl of Aboyne, etc.? He was wearing a different, even gaudier kilt this evening . . . and after I'd had two drinks, I said: "What a fortunate man you are, to have a choice of plaids. What's this dilly?"

"The Comyn dress plaid. It doesna please you, cousin?"

"Oh, it's infinitely pleasing—but aren't you afraid you'll scare the game?"

"One doesna wear a dress plaid for hunting, cousin. 'Tis worn only indoors, for special occasions."

"Yes, that's what I thought, and I still say you'll scare the game."

"You're not looking in the least frightened, cousin," Sholto returned, studying me carefully. He chuckled. "So ye've no head for heights, but once on the ground

80

you've your wits about you and a tongue to match."

It was a peculiar evening, not helpful for making a decision. The atmosphere was oddly harmonious, although conversation was minimal. For the first time we were relaxed together, capable of companionable silence. I was beginning to think it'd work out after all; we were over the hump of getting to know each other. The Laird was lost in thought—planning for the mill, I guessed, or the possible coup of the Campbells. And Annis undoubtedly was concerned with the houseparty details. I'd no clue to Sholto's thoughts, but he seemed happy enough.

There were no pipes that night; we thought along uninterrupted until dessert, when Annis asked: "Will you want the local people asked for dinner Thursday, David, or merely for the dance?"

"Thursday?" Sholto repeated. "You're planning a shoot this year then?"

"Years since we've done the pretty, I want Sable to experience the whole thing since she's here," David smiled at me.

"I see. You've picked a good year. The coverts are as full as they can hold," Sholto remarked. "How many blinds?"

"With the house full, we'll need them all."

"Four beaters, eight dogs," Sholto nodded. "I can spare two men and three dogs from Comynhaugh."

"Had you not meant to be at Strathmuir, then?" Annis was definitely disturbed, but surely after twenty years the Laird knew how to manage a shoot?

"I hadn't really thought, Annis, but assuming David would be away, I'd a vague plan to shoot my own coverts for a change."

"You've not made your own party?" Annis sighed with relief when Sholto shook his head. "You'll come to us instead? I don't know how we would have managed without you . . . so many people, so much to arrange. . . ." Her voice trailed away.

"Of course, I'll be here," Sholto said soothingly. "I'd no idea our cousin's stay was to be so protracted, but if she's the occasion for a major hoop-la, I wouldn't miss it for the world," he added drily. "I'll engage ye for that first reel, cousin. Ye do reel, do ye not?"

"Constantly," I assured him, finishing the inevitable *flan*. His tone was pleasant enough but his eyes were cold. He still wanted me gone and was jolted to discover I'd be staying on for days to come. But I still wasn't sure that I'd stay, especially if Sholto meant to make my life miserable. It occurred to me that my indecision was really concerned with Lord Aboyne, who was alternately fun and infuriation . . . and why the hell should I let him get away with it?

No matter what spicy tidbit existed in the records that he'd rather I didn't find, I'd gotten to like David Kirby-Gordon. Well—not exactly like, but appreciate. He'd been polite even before learning of Aunt Agnes. As we followed Annis to the salon for demitasse, I made up my mind: I would stay, say nothing, and keep my nose very clean.

Sipping my coffee, I knew it was *point non plus* anyway, what with invitations already out, Annis making plans and Sholto pressed into service. I didn't like being used, even for a plan that I could approve personally . . . but never mind; let David make the pitch his own way. I'd have a film, a bit of fun. . . .

"You're silent, cousin. Was the day too tiring for a

city lass?" Sholto asked.

"Only thinking of my photographs," I said, turning to the Laird. "David, MacDanald asked for a few of the best color shots for his window display. I thought if they were only views everyone already knew, you wouldn't object."

"Of course. Though I'd like to see what you mean to give him."

"I put a special on these rolls—they'll be done before I leave, so you can choose." I could wire the processor to send them here instead of to Cascadine. . . .

"Good, good! I confess I'm anxious to see the results. She must have taken a dozen rolls, Annis! Everytime I turned she was reloading. Amazing!"

"You were actually atop the fortalice, Sable?" Annis shuddered. "The only time I went up was years ago when we first married—you recall, David? I thought I should never get down again. A most unpleasant experience!"

"Oh, you're so right, Annis," I said. "I got up easily enough. David was very clever at strapping the cameras so they wouldn't hamper me, and I shot six full rolls—but Sholto had to carry me down."

He emptied his liqueur glass at a gulp. "What had ye planned on doing if I hadna been there, cousin?"

"I'd have crawled down bass-ackwards, of course," I said sweetly, ignoring Annis's uncomprehending frown.

"Och, a pity I came." Sholto refilled his brandy glass. "That would have been a sight worth seeing, cousin. If I let ye up again, will ye agree to demonstrate?"

"Are ye so desperate for the sight of a female, cousin?" I asked. "I'll assure ye I'm nothing out o' the common. Ye should go to Lunnon Town for a sight o' the Windmill."

"You've a very good accent, Sable," Annis approved, "a real feel for the burr."

"That she has," Sholto agreed, "as well as where to place it. I wouldna trust this one with a claymore, I'll tell ye." His shoulders shook silently. "Och, cousin— the *Windmill?* Did ye present yersel' to the manager, ye'd have star billing, clothes and a' . . ."

Damn the man for needling me again. I was too mad even to blush. Star billing at a burleycue? "I doubt it," I told him calmly. "I'm far too dainty. Ye have to remember the laddie in the last seat o' the top row paid his money. He wants to see, too."

Sholto's blue eyes sparkled dangerously above the liqueur glass. "I was always one for the front row. The Comyns are fastidious, ye ken?"

"A bunch of stage door Johnnies?" I asked, shocked. "Tchk, and supposed to be pillars o' the Kirk? What would the Dominie say?"

David suddenly came to. "Oh, perfectly acceptable for titles to marry musical comedy stars, Sable—June, Adele Astaire, Beatrice Lillie," he assured me seriously.

Annis chimed in, *"No one* would ever have taken your grandmother for a Gaiety Girl, Sholto! She was absolutely accepted everywhere."

Sholto was waiting to see what I'd say. "Of course, once she'd abandoned 'trade,'" I murmured, finishing my brandy with bravado. There was a minute's pause. I could sense incomprehension from David and Annis. Sholto finished his own brandy, banged the glass on the tray and laughed until he was limp in his chair.

"Eh, Sable—cousin," he said, gasping between

snorts and chuckles, "ye'll be the death o' me—and I've to endure ye for near a week?" He shook his head, struggling to his feet. "I'm no' sure I'll survive. I mun' look to ma heir, whoever he is."

"But you know quite well," Annis protested literally. "He's somebody named Lennox."

I looked at Sholto with absolute horror. *No,* it couldn't be . . . my father! I remembered Aunt Agnes's oblique warning, and Sholto's faint twitch of the lips was confirmation enough. . . . I sat, stunned, barely able to nod my head when he said goodnight. . . . David finished his coffee and excused himself for a bit of work in the study. . . . Annis decreed bed at eleven. . . .

It would have to be straightened out, of course. Oh, why hadn't Aunt Agnes briefed me? I got into night clothes and walked back and forth in my room. No wonder Sholto didn't like me. Could I convince him that I hadn't known, that I wasn't sent to spy out the land? No wonder he'd been coldly contemptuous when I was blowing off about Mrs. Ware's wealth! What need could *her* nephew have for a title and estates?

I could feel tears of shame rolling down my cheeks. I'd no one to blame but myself, really. Aunt Agnes had never dreamed I'd be invited to stay with the family. Nor did she know that Sholto was the resident estate agent and might misinterpret my request to use the files. She'd given me a clue, but I'd got it too late, after I'd already done every blessed thing as wrong as possible. I'd been flip, I'd sassed him, I'd blown up at him. . . . Oh, what could Sholto think of his heir's daughter?

My only hope was Lord Everard and Lady Jean.

Whether or not they knew Daddy was Sholto's heir, they certainly knew that I was unaware of that. I decided to post a post-script to my letter.

I grabbed my flashlight and opened my door. The halls were dark and the house silent. Quietly I found my way to the main stairs, and hesitated. Was it my imagination—or had there been motion below, a figure receding along the hall to the servants' wing? I listened but now I heard nothing. It was probably Andrew closing for the night. The torch picked out my letter lying on the hall table. Again I hesitated. After a moment, I whisked downstairs, seized the letter and . . . sensed an odd dampness in my fingers. I raced back to my room, closed the door, and waited until I'd caught my breath before letting the fact sink in: The envelope had just been steamed open and resealed.

Chapter 6

As I sank into the fireside chair and stared at the letter, I was conscious of a definite throb of fright. There was no mistake. When I inserted a gentle fingernail at the edge, the flap peeled up at once; the glue hadn't had time to set. Who—and why?

David? Wondering whether I'd backed his invitation? Or Sholto, wondering whether I'd complained of his behavior to his godfather? Neither man would anticipate an afterthought from Cousin Sable when she'd retired for the night. If I'd been two seconds earlier, my torch would have caught whoever was replacing the letter.

I threw a shovelful of coals on the dwindling fire, lit a cigarette and added the postscript: "Unless politically inexpedient or truly impossible because of prior commitments, I beg you to accept David's invitation!" From my window, the Laird's suite was dark. I picked up my torch, softly stole out and down the stairs to lay the letter on the hall table. In less than a minute I was back, leaning thankfully against my locked door while my breathing steadied.

Whatever was going on, I meant to get to the bottom of it. I had the drop on them. I knew they were spying on me; they didn't know I knew. I would diddle them with sweetness and light. I'd write dozens of postcards, "Wish you were here," to every person in my address book. I'd write up the diary fulsomely, burbling over the slightest detail.

And I'd take anything at all private directly to Strathbogie to mail when I dispatched my film. On the other hand, why should it be necessary? What possible threat could I present to these two men that they should want to keep me under such surveillance? How close were the Liverpool water rat and the Oxford-bred aristocrat? I thought they'd be united for the good of the Clan.

Was Daddy really Sholto's heir? I smothered a yawn. Then I sat upright with shock. Of course he was, and Sholto was David Kirby-Gordon's heir. Which meant Daddy was in line not only for two earldoms but a marquessate as well—unless Sholto married and got a son.

Daddy would hate it. But if he repudiated the titles, they would go to my brother Charles, who'd like them even less. I could visualize the clutch of nobility bouncing downward through my family, winding up at Zed, because he was ten minutes younger than Zachary. . . . All the same, it really wasn't funny.

Why hadn't Sholto married? I couldn't make myself believe he was carrying a torch for Annis. Unwillingly, I remembered the warm strength of his arms, the good clean smell of him this afternoon. . . . The man was madly attractive for all he was forty-ish. Why hadn't some woman snapped him up long since? Why was he content to play second fiddle to a slum boy with whom he'd nothing in common mentally?

Which brought me back to the record room that no one had been allowed to use in twenty years. Sleepily, I remembered that a number of titled families had been ruined by death duties when heirs were killed a day or two apart during the war. Could there have been an heir ahead of David Kirby who hadn't died before the old Laird? Two lots of death duties would certainly have finished the estate, if David had found nothing but land and moribund business interests.

If that was what it was—a pact between Sholto and David to bilk tax collectors—I was for it. But if there had been someone before David, wouldn't Aunt Agnes have known? Not necessarily; she'd said she knew less about the female lines. That was why I was here.

The alternative was a spicy tale concerning one of David's ancestors. Where Sholto could laugh about a chorus-girl grandmother, David would be ashamed. I was curious as a cat and naughtily determined to dig it out for Aunt Agnes's amusement; neither of us would ever tell, but it'd be fun to know.

Two thoughts skimmed across my mind as I was falling asleep: Ironically, the wariness of both men had caused my suspicions. Had they taken me at face value, I'd have gotten what Aunt Agnes wanted and probably never gone near the record room again. I might have left—or stayed to enjoy the intrigue of this party.

Which led to thought two: For a ball, I would need a gown. . . .

*　　　*　　　*

If I needed confirmation, I had it next morning when I entered the record room.

"David had to go over to Aberdeen," Sholto said politely, "which is my chance to work up estate records. I hope I won't disturb you, cousin? These blasted forms!"

"Not in the least," I said, equally polite. He was right behind me while I hunted out the card references, insistent on trotting up the ladder for bound volumes on the top shelf. "Please," I protested. "I'll feel it's I who disturbs you if you stop work to fetch and carry for me. You forget I'm quite used to ladders and top shelves."

"I've not forgotten—nor the way librarians waste time browsing. Ye'll get up there, and ye'll be looking at the next and the next, until ye'll never be finished." He grinned wickedly, setting my books firmly on the work table. "Time enough to browse when ye've got what ye came for, cousin."

Oh, yeah? I settled meekly to work, wondering when that moment would arrive. More than ever sure I wasn't to be let at the files unchaperoned, I concentrated on the remaining dates and was through in short order. Sholto was still laboriously filling out his forms. "Can't those be done on a typewriter?"

He nodded. "But it's accurate work, and I can't handle the machine."

"I can," I said, "unless it's confidential." He looked up at me, pen suspended in his fingers. "I'm finished and available."

"Nothing confidential. Ye wouldn't understand farm production figures, anyway; you're a city lass." He smiled suddenly. "Would you really not mind, Sable?"

"Of course not. Call it a house present."

"I'll reward ye," he announced mischievously. "If we're done before luncheon, I'll take ye to the spinney for the best shots of the river. How's that?"

"Not if I have to walk there," I told him austerely, remembering the distance as seen from the fortalice.

"Of course not, we'll go in the jeep." He raised his eyebrows. "I'm saving your feet for that reel, come Thursday, cousin."

He rolled out the typing stand. "I don't know what shape it's in," he said dubiously, whipping off the cover to reveal a fairly new Royal Standard.

"Give me a sheet of scratch paper and we'll see." I did a few "quick brown foxes" and said, "It could use some type cleaner; otherwise it's ding-ho."

"Where'd you learn that?" he asked, hunting in a supply cabinet and producing a bottle.

"My oldest brother was with Chennault."

"Charles, eh?" he murmured absently, rooting out carbon paper while I vigorously scrubbed the keys.

How did Sholto know my brother's name? "It's not really true, is it—that my father's your heir?"

"At the moment. Didn't you know?"

I shook my head violently. "Of *course* not, or I wouldn't—"

"Have come?" he finished calmly, tossing the paper toward me. "That would have been our grave loss, cousin. Shall we begin?"

An hour later he was signing dozens of sheets while I directed envelopes and folded enclosures. "Luncheon is served, milord," Andrew said from the doorway.

"We'll be right there, Andrew. I hope you've enough stamps for this lot." Sholto briskly thumped the final flap and stood up, shuffling the mail together. "I played on our cousin's sympathies to operate the machine, and everything's finished."

"Do a'done now!" Andrew forgot formality in his amazement.

Sholto laughed. "A fortunate day Miss Lennox came to us, Andrew, and ye'll spread the word I'll be a human being tonight instead of a bear with a sore head."

"Happy they'll be to know it," Andrew said tartly, taking the pile of letters. "Ye'll not know what ye've done for Strathmuir this day, mistress! These forms—four times a year his lordship is intol'rable for a full twa days, the way all stay out of his path!"

"A pity she must ever leave us, eh, Andrew?" Sholto hugged me lightly, turned me to the door.

"Aye," the old butler eyed us with a twitch of his shaggy eyebrows, "I ha' been thinkin' the same since fairst I saw her."

"Are you finding what you wanted, Sable?"

"Yes, thank you, Annis. I finished this morning."

"She even finished all my work, too. I promised to repay by taking her and her cameras to the south spinney. Come with us?"

"Oh—so many arrangements . . . I'm waiting to hear about the music. Everything local is booked; they're asking Hylton's, but if they send, it's extra rooms," she sighed, "and ten to one they'll refuse to eat with the staff."

"Or vice versa," Sholto said irrepressibly. "Nonsense, Annis! No use waiting by a telephone, better

92

have some fresh air. You haven't been to the spinney in a long while."

He was no more anxious to avoid a tête-à-tête than I! "Is that where the blueberries are? Steenie predicts a bumper crop."

She brightened at once. "Yes, I really should see how many jars and pots will be needed."

"Wear something colorful, so I can have pictures of the Laird's Lady on her native heath," I cajoled.

"It isn't a heath, Sable," she said. "A spinney is a coppice."

I didn't dare look at Sholto; I could feel him quivering at the other side of the table. When I could control my voice I said, "Whatever it is, I'd like pictures—and if I can secretary for Sholto, I can do the same for you. Except that first, I must somehow acquire a proper evening gown. Is there any shop in Aberdeen, Annis?"

"Holt or Shockley," she said automatically and frowned. "You haven't a ball gown, Sable?"

"One doesn't travel with them, unless alerted beforehand," I said. "So if I'm to do you credit, I must purchase a gown."

"Ye're too modest, cousin," Sholto flattered. "Ye'd do us sufficient credit did ye wear one of my gaudy kilts."

"I'd still have to drive to Aberdeen for feminine underpinnings." I ignored the sudden splutter into his tankard of ale. "So I might as well buy a new dress while I'm about it."

"I'll drive ye, and approve your purchase!" he stated.

"I've a fancy to keep ye in suspense till the grand moment."

93

"Tchk, this American independence," he fretted. "How will ye know what to buy without a man to guide ye, lass?"

"It's enough if you tell me what you have in mind, milord, and let the result be a surprise."

Sholto cocked his head. "Something green," he decided. "Clinging, but with an ample skirt. Else ye'll trip in the reel."

"Are you a stock size, Sable?" Annis asked, still perturbed. "I'm not sure we mightn't do better to telephone Fragonard's in London, there'd be time enough for air delivery if you've an idea what you want?"

"Sholto says it must be green and clinging. I expect I can find something in Aberdeen, Annis, and I rather like to try things on. If I went tomorrow morning, I'd be back for luncheon."

She looked at me carefully. "If you'd rather. . . . Green," she murmured, "yes, a good color for you. Sholto has excellent taste."

"Naturally. What else from the grandson of a Gaiety Girl?"

Sholto tossed his napkin on the table and stood up, laughing heartily. "Leave Sable to find her own dress, I'll be ready for you at two o'clock."

As he was going out the door Andrew came in hastily. "The Laird wishes to speak with ye, milord. Shall I put it through to the record room?"

"Please, Andrew. . . ."

I changed to slacks, rubber-soled shoes, readied my cameras and dashed off a dozen "wish you were heres."

The visitor cards of Strathmuir were stodgy, floridly colored. I'd get a better shot for David to use when the current stock was finished. Standing idly on the front steps, I realized suddenly that I'd need a special session with Ranald MacDanald if I were to get a complete film of the shoot!

I'd only one motion camera; two minutes would never be enough, no matter how carefully I filmed or spliced. The angles of view would differ, the dogs, the birds in flight. . . .

"What distresses ye, cousin?"

I hadn't even heard the jeep pull up. I looked at Sholto and said, despairingly, "Unless Ranald Mac-Danald has a 16-mm Bolex to lend me, this whole thing is an absolute waste of time."

"Ye came only to make motion pictures?"

"No, of course not," I said crossly. "You know I meant to leave today—but David's got me lassoed with this party, and if I've got to stay, I want a decent film of the shoot—and I've only the one camera."

"Tchk, a bad mistake," he agreed. "I suppose you thought the still cameras would be enough to record your heritage."

That did it! He really did think I'd come to photograph Strathmuir so Daddy could see what he'd inherit? I was down the front steps before I even realized I was moving—and smacked the Earls of Aboyne and Sutherland with all the force of a left arm that had won three silver tennis cups for Bryn Mawr. "Dammit," I said furiously, "if you think any decent American wants this, think again. And if it bothers you so much, why don't you get married and produce a few sons?"

95

He massaged his cheek gently. "Aye," he agreed, "I'd been thinking o' that very thing recently."

"Well, do something about it, will you?"

"Mayhap I will," he said, with an odd smile, "if only to avert another o'your haymakers, cousin."

I could feel myself growing red. "I'm sorry," I said in a very small voice, looking determinedly at my toes, "but if you think I was sent to survey the terrain, I wasn't. Daddy would simply loathe having to be a Laird. He's happy to pieces living with Mummy in Georgetown and masterminding at NASA."

"No doubt—but there's Charles and your five other brothers, some already married with sons." He shook his head admiringly, *"Dhu,* ye're a hearty lot, ye Lennoxes!"

"Sad to realize the Comyns are no longer their equal," I flared, and felt a firm hand forcing my chin up until I'd no choice but to face him.

"Why will ye entice me into teasing ye, cousin?" He chuckled softly, then suddenly became serious. "Should anything happen to me, your father will find a successor," Sholto's lips twitched. "And it's the measure of his value to Uncle Sam that your government will pay the death duties to retain him. Now, does that content ye, lass?"

"Yes, and no," I said, when I'd grasped the implications. "Couldn't you please get married, so Daddy won't be bothered at all?"

Before he could say anything, Annis came down the steps. "Sorry to delay you, but Lady Atherton phoned; the speaker for the Woman's Institute has failed. It's either find a substitute or cancel," she sighed distractedly, "and with the notices out, it's far too late for that." She'd reached the bottom step. "Sable!" she breathed thankfully. "Of course! Why didn't I think of it at once? You won't mind saying a few words, will you?"

"Saying a few words about what?"

"Oh, anything," Annis waved her hand. "Tell them about America. Film stars are best, but anything will do." She pushed me into the jeep between herself and Sholto, and we were soon bouncing forward toward the farm track to the spinney.

"But I've never made a speech in my life, Annis!"

"Not really a speech," Sholto said quietly. "It's only a little talk to a bunch of women who like to hear about something new to them, Sable. You could tell about your work. The films that helped in Dahomey—they'd like that. I expect you've plenty of similar stories."

I was torn between pleasure at his perception and stage-fright. Of course there were other stories; would they interest Scottish farm wives?

"Don't go so quickly, Sholto," Annis complained. "I can't see the vines."

"Sorry." We crawled at snail's pace until she said, "Stop! Tchk, I *knew* there were more black raspberries, Steenie never picks the bushes clean." She was out to the road the instant Sholto braked.

He calmly fished about in the back to produce a plaited rush basket. I took it away from him. "Standard equipment?" I asked and nipped out to thrust it at Annis.

"Thank you, my dear." In two seconds Annis was busily stripping the canes, while I dashed back for a camera. Sholto lounged at the wheel, observing my shots of the Lady Annis Kirby-Gordon culling black raspberries. I finished with the photographs before she finished with the raspberries, and since it was obvious we wouldn't proceed until the harvest was complete, I tucked the camera into the jeep and joined her.

"I really think that's all for today. Come on, Annis— let's inspect the blueberries. . . ."

Sholto produced another basket for the blueberries, and I took more pictures of the Lady Annis gathering fresh fruits. Luckily the major crop wasn't due for another week, and eventually we came to a stop under a huge shade tree.

"Now, cousin, if ye'll bring the cameras, I'll conduct ye," Sholto said. "Annis?"

"I think I'll wait here," she said, nibbling a few raspberries. "Don't be too long, or we'll be late for tea."

The view was all Sholto'd promised. I took a full roll, reloaded, while he rambled about in the underbrush behind me. "You're satisfied with the angle?"

"Yes—except I can't get a shot of the mill. There's a branch in the way."

"I'll set ye on my shoulder," he decided, and before I could draw a breath I was aloft. I leaned against a tree trunk for balance while he steadied my legs. I was momentarily flustered, but the view was too superb to be lost for miss-ishness. I bracketed the roll and said, "Thanks, it was perfect, Sholto. You can let me down."

He seemed not to hear. "It's a pretty scene," he murmured, "the mill and all. . . . I suppose David told ye his plans; he'll be wanting capital from Mrs. Ware, no doubt."

"Plans?"

Sholto swung me to the ground so suddenly I gasped. "He told ye, else how did ye know of the mill?" he stated calmly. "'Tis all right, lass, I'll not press your confidence—but that was what ye were discussing on the fortalice." He narrowed his eyes with a half-smile of satisfaction. "And the reason David was hugging ye when I arrived. 'Tis a project dear to his heart!" Sholto rubbed his hands together briskly. "Take the last pictures, cousin, else we'll be late for tea."

I concentrated on the view. Sholto had figured the whole thing from no more than my mention of the mill? David had said Sholto'd offered his smokehouses for a trial—obviously he approved of the project. Impulsively I turned—about to say, if *he* thought it wise, I'd break the family rule of non-pressure to explain to Aunt Agnes. I had my lips open but I closed them and said nothing. . . .

Sholto was half-turned from me, leaning against one of the big trees, looking down into the flowing waters of the Deveron that were racing blue-green ripples. The last low-slanting rays of afternoon sun filtered through the leaves, lighting his face softly. He was wholly unaware of me. He was a man lost in masculine dreams that made his chin arrogant, his lips firm, his complete profile strong yet kindly.

He was quite beautiful: rugged, dependable, undefeatable.

I held my breath, finished both rolls of film as swiftly as possible. On the final shot he caught me. "What are ye doing?"

"You were so perfectly posed, I couldn't resist." I apologized, feeling my heart turn over at the blue flash in his eyes.

99

"A waste of your film, cousin," he shrugged, taking my elbow and turning back to the jeep.

"Yes, it would have been more effectively if you'd been in a kilt," I agreed, breathlessly trying to match his long strides.

He dropped my arm when we reached level ground and easily outdistanced me. Soon he was leaning over Annis, who was asleep over the half-empty basket of raspberries. "Wake up, ma bonnie," his tender voice reached me quite clearly.

"Wha'? Where am I?" she said blearily, opening her eyes and smiling at him suddenly. "Sholto," she murmured, closing her eyes again.

"Slip in from the driver's door," Sholto told me. "Put your arm around her, Sable; hold her steady till she wakes."

Silently I obeyed. She sagged against me limply while we bounced over the rutted farm track.

I watched Sholto's strong fingers gripping the wheel firmly, competently, fully in control. I felt hypnotized, close to tears. Those hands were so like Jeremy's. . . . They could grip the stick of a plane as wonderfully as they could caress a woman's hand. I felt hypnotized, close to tears. . . . Jeremy's hands had been fully in control, too, that time . . . until the moment a drunken teenager sideswiped him at 80 mph. . . . Until the very last moment. . . .

Chapter 7

Annis was awake by the time we bounced into the garage court. She crawled out, smothering a gigantic yawn, while I picked up the fruit baskets. "Thanks, Sholto."

"My pleasure, cousin." He headed the jeep toward its stall, and I caught up with Annis at the rear door.

"Sable, would you mind having tea alone? I'd rather like mine upstairs—David won't be back till dinner." Flushed with sleep and smiling, Annis looked the pretty young girl again for a moment. "They'll bring yours where you like—iced, if you wish. . . ."

"I think, instead of tea, I'll take the film to the post and talk to MacDanald."

Annis shook her head. "Early closing day, he won't be open." She yawned again and disappeared along a side passage.

Darn, I'd forgotten the British irregular half-days that vary exasperatingly from one locality to another. Was it worthwhile to drive down merely to mail? I wandered along to the pantry and set the fruit baskets before Andrew, who took one glance at me and asked, "What's amiss?"

"I'd a favor to ask MacDanald, but I forgot about early closing."

"He'll be proud to be disturbed. I'll just place the call for ye, mistress. . . ."

Twenty minutes later I was having tea with the MacDanalds in their garden. "Sorry I'm not properly dressed. Lord Aboyne took us to the spinney," I said anxiously. "Oh, dear—I shouldn't even have come to the post looking like this."

Ranald's lips twitched. "I'll no' say I'd ask everyone, but ye'll be more formal clad than ye'll see," he remarked, ushering me through the shop. "Bess, here's Miss Lennox, cousin to the Laird."

I glanced at the violent purple bikini scantily concealing Mrs. MacDanald and at her appalled expression. Her husband chuckled. *"Men!"* I said. "I said I wasn't decently dressed—and he deliberately brings me to see how much more comfortable you are! I apologize for the intrusion."

"Nay, I'm glad to meet ye, however informal." She pulled herself together and offered tea and sandwiches. "Ye'll be talking to the Institute, I hear? What'll be the subject?"

I choked into the cup. "However did you hear so soon?"

"Lady Annis tells Lady Atherton, who tells me not five minutes past," she grinned. "I'm secretary, 'tis my duty to post notices, ye ken? So what'll ye tell us?"

"Lord Aboyne says I should talk about my job. I'm head of a photographic library in New York, but I've never made a speech. . . ."

"Ye'll be a refreshing novelty," she assured me. "Photographs, now—what sort, why d'ye keep them, what d'ye do with them?" I tried the Dahomey story and concluded that if the rest of the ladies were equally quick of mind, I'd have no trouble. "'Tis fascinating," she said finally. "We'll like to hear about it, Miss Lennox, and dinna worry about speech-making. We're only a group of women like yersel'."

I drove back to Strathmuir with not one but two movie cameras borrowed from stock ("Pish, tush, ye'll not abuse them—forbye ye'll gie us a print?"). I was anxious to make notes for my maiden speech. Six-thirty, ninety free minutes—I hopped in and out of the shower, dressed quickly and began scrawling notes on Strathmuir crested stationery. I yearned for a type-writer.

I wouldn't be allowed to use the record room unchaperoned—I'd forgotten that—but the machine wasn't heavy. Trotting down for pre-dinner drinks, I thought to myself that the instant David knew why I wanted it, he'd hoick it up to my room himself! And so he might have, except that he wasn't home. "Gone to Liverpool for a special meeting, back tomorrow," Sholto said. "Why so downcast, cousin?"

"I wanted the typewriter. I thought, if you'd excuse me after dinner, Annis, I'd outline ideas for the Institute."

"You can't work in the record room," Sholto stated. "The temperature control system makes it too chilly at night, ye'd be frozen in five minutes. Andrew, have the machine and stand taken to Miss Lennox's room, please."

Clever! Very neat! I was not surprised when Lord Aboyne escorted us to the salon for demitasse, and made his excuses. "No coffee tonight, Annis, thanks. Good luck with the outline, cousin—I'll see you tomorrow."

"Not till afternoon, I'm for Aberdeen to buy that dress."

"Green and clinging," he warned, smiling wickedly. "Mind now, if ye come back with anything else, I'll have it returned and buy the thing myself."

"You're determined to be a Regency buck, aren't you? Green and clinging, cross my heart and hope to die!" I promised solemnly.

I didn't go to Aberdeen after all. A note from Annis on the early tea tray: "See me before you start, I have thought of something."

"Is Lady Annis awake, should I go along now?"

"Aye—I'll take your tea whiles ye talk," Nellie answered.

I threw on my robe and padded after Nellie. I found Annis wrapped in a maribou jacket and staring at me owlishly over huge black-framed spectacles. "Good morning, Sable, did you sleep well? Nellie, bring me that box, please. . . . I suddenly remembered," she said, removing the box top, "Aberdeen shops are well enough for a provincial city, but not likely you'd find anything really suitable for an important party." She pulled aside tissue paper, spilling a flood of vibrant green silk over the coverlet. I caught my breath delightedly.

It was the color of creme de menthe, soft and slithery. Annis squinted reflectively. "Yes, it's perfect for you, Sable—d'you like it? Mrs. Frame and Nellie are very competent seamstresses. We could make the gown here—unless you wanted something fussy."

I shook my head. "I wanted something plain, with a full skirt."

"Then it's settled. Nellie, take the silk and ask Miss Lennox what she'll want, please."

"Aye, milady." Nellie's eyes sparkled with plesure as she tucked the silk into its box and went away.

"You'll let me pay you, Annis? It's exactly the color I wanted, I'd never have found it short of London. . . ."

"No, no, offer Nellie a couple of guineas if you wish, but it's not necessary; she loves to sew and actually she's extremely clever," Annis said.

"But that's yards and yards of very expensive fabric," I protested uncomfortably. "Are you sure you want to give it to me?"

"Yes," she said with unexpected humor. "It was given to me—some business associate of David's, either currying favor or repaying one, I forget. It's far too strong a shade for me. I must have had it laid by for three years—lucky I remembered."

"Well—I can't thank you enough, Annis."

She smiled faintly. "For giving you something I can't use, that will enable you to do credit to David? You'll be electrifying!"

"I hope so, you've both been so very kind to me, Annis."

"You've deserved it. You're amazingly companionable, my dear. I never knew David to take to anyone so quickly," she said surprisingly, "but we've all enjoyed your visit, Sable. Now, run away and consult with Nellie. I'll see you at luncheon."

While I dressed for formal breakfast, I pondered. I was beginning to feel like a weather vane, blown this way and that every few hours. Both her words and actions convinced me that this humorless stupid woman had not jilted the Earl of Aboyne for a softer berth, but had married for love. Never mind what the world thought—I'd found David Kirby-Gordon not unattractive on closer acquaintance. To Annis Richmond, a half-starved overworked young girl struggling ignorantly for survival during the years she ought to have been in college, he was probably a veritable Lochinvar.

To a stupid woman, his energetic go-getter personality would have been irresistible. Because she lived nearby, Annis probably even knew that there was nothing to the estate but the old Laird's tangled affairs; she'd still taken David. She must have been invaluable at first, thriftily bottling and preserving, providing correct social training. But once the financial heat was off, she'd nothing more to offer. Poor girl, I thought soberly, she could only continue to do what she could do: overstock the storeroom, cope with a huge houseparty at a moment's notice, give away a hundred dollars' worth of exquisite silk so a distant cousin would do credit to her husband. . . .

He'd only married her for expediency. He no longer shared her bed and he spent most of his time away "on business." Cynically I thought it would have been no different if she'd had a son; David would still have been bored, found his fun elsewhere. That's where he was right now, no doubt. He probably assumed from his phone talk with Sholto last night that I'd gone to Aberdeen. Couldn't he wait even a week for his jolly?

But I hadn't gone to Aberdeen.

"Is Lord Aboyne around?"

Andrew shook his head. "He was early about, collecting the papers from the record room and has gone to Comynhaugh for the morning. Is there something ye want?"

"No, thanks. I only wanted to ask if I could go up to the farther fields, but it can wait."

The instant the butler disappeared, I nipped along to the record room. Sholto had left it unlocked! I chuckled silently, flipping through the file cards and sparing sincere admiration for the superb job: hand-written cards in bold black India ink, about 1840–50; spidery hand-written cards circa 1870–80; in, around and about were neatly typed cards replacing originals that must have grown too illegible.

I'd settled in my own mind that a good point of departure would be that gypsy girl who married the first David Kirby . . . and in fifteen minutes I had it! Via Lady Constance Gordon (1775–1831) I learned that when Carmela turned up at Strathmuir, there were not one, but *two* baby boys!

One was two-and-a-half, the image of his father; the other was six months, with an unfortunate resemblance to his mother. However, there was no getting around Wellington's signature on her wedding lines.

I wondered why Aunt Agnes hadn't known of the older child. Was this the diary she hadn't had time to finish? I concentrated, growing used to faded ink and Spencerian script until I could skip the dull bits. The boys were George and David, and once Carmela had flown, Lady Constance was more and more "catched by my grandnevvys." She expatiated on their quick intelligence, bright eyes, loving ways—until tragedy struck.

In 1818, George developed some sort of feveer and died.

The old lady filled pages with sentimental gush over his little soul ascending to await her at the pearly gates—but there was still David, and I was now thoroughly confused. Which one *was* David: legit or illegit? I went word by word through the diary three times, and damned if I could tell which kid had died!

By implication, though, I'd a naughty hunch this was IT: the legit had expired, and David Kirby was descended from a technical bastard. Oh, wouldn't he hate *that* made public! I replaced the diary and thought suddenly, "That's strange—David's eyes are light gray, but in the wedding picture his parents both had brown eyes." Impulsively, I hunted up Mendelian Law in the dictionary, but it was all plants and botany. I was still certain I'd heard brown-eyed parents couldn't produce light-eyed children—unless . . . there were light-eyed ancestors!

Presumably the original David Kirby had been a light-eyed fair-skinned Gordon; could that heritage have endured for a hundred years? I had the vague impression Mary's eyes were *light* brown in Aunt Agnes's photograph; considering the lousy tint job, perhaps they should have been gray—because there was no doubt at all about David Kirby's father. I remembered him clearly: pure wild Rom, black eyes, black hair . . . exactly the sort to be bumped off in a saloon fracas.

There's one thing about being a librarian: you know how to use a file. Swiftly I got out everything pertaining to Strathmuir between 1814 and 1820. There were other references to the two children, but nowhere was there any definite identification of which was which. It was exactly the sort of tantalizing puzzle to intrigue a researcher!

I traced every reference painstakingly, and with the exception of one letter that was marked on the file card "Illegible due to water damage, discarded 1935," I found nothing. It *had* to be those two babies . . . unless it was even farther back. It took another hour, but eventually I knew beyond a shadow of a doubt that Eleanor, her three daughters plus all their progeny, were completely legitimate. Until that extra baby boy in 1815.

I put everything away very neatly—even cleaned out the ashtray to leave no trace of my presence. Then I slipped quietly out to the hall and up to my bedroom, grinning to myself all the while. This had to be what the Laird didn't want me to find. Although there was nothing definitive in the files, somehow he knew he was descended from the illegitimate baby, and wanted no questions raised.

The weather vane in my mind veered about again. I was no longer entirely on David's side. He wasn't very smart, I thought drily. Granted his wife bored him to death, he was stupid to judge other women by Annis— and that was what he'd done. He'd put himself out to charm and please, first with an intimate business conversation on the fortalice, then with the major flattery of a grouse-shoot and ball in my honor. It had never occurred to him I might not be fooled by such attention.

It was the Laird then who'd read my diary and inspected my letter to the Campbells. It could never have been Sholto. It was not his nature to spy surreptitiously, even to protect the Laird. It was David who was the sneaky personality, who'd steamed open my letter—and finding nothing but pleasant words, had felt secure in having made the correct impression. *Yon's an oily conniver. . . .*

The more fool he, I thought coldly. He'd allowed far too much time for me to gain a perspective. Left alone with Annis, I'd learned that she loved her husband. And I had realized the impropriety of his tiny scornful sniping remarks to me, a virtual stranger.

I was suddenly anti-David. He'd made a contract that suited him; the least he could do, when he no longer needed Annis, was to treat her with courtesy. It wouldn't cost all that much effort. Sholto could do it for auld lang syne. He could live here, suppress kindly laughter at her lack of humor, take along rush baskets for fruit, and call Annis "my bonnie." It was not undying passion, but gentle protection for a girl he'd known all his life.

I felt a warm rush of admiration for the real aristocrat, who'd shield a stupid woman and maintain uneasy peace between husband and wife. I'd have bet Sholto could control David even when he threatened to be outrageous. Still, it was a major outlay of life and time that he should have used for a family of his own.

There was a tap at the door. Nellie sidled in shyly

with an armful of the latest fashion magazines. "I've marked the ones we can easily copy, but if there's another ye fancy, we'll contrive."

I looked at what she'd chosen and nearly fainted! Any one of them would have run a thousand bucks or more. Nellie was excited; dying to get started. There was one in a double-page spread in *Elle*. It clung, it swirled about a red-haired model with fantastic eye makeup. The dress was violet chiffon, but there was no doubt—that was the style. "Could you really copy that, Nellie?"

"O'course," she chortled. "It's that ye'd like? 'Tis the very one Mrs. Frame and I picked for ye! If ye'll let me take the measurements, we'll be well away this verra afternoon . . ."

I ate luncheon alone after all. Annis had gone to consult with Lady Atherton about the Women's Institute, and there was no sign of Sholto. "Have ye seen the pattern for my dress, Andrew?"

"That I have. It'll suit ye fine."

"It'd cost a thousand dollars in New York. What's the very most I can give Nellie without offense, Andrew?"

He pursed his lips. "Ye'll wait till ye see how she turns it out," he said cautiously. "Then I'll tell ye. Will ye want more ice for the tea, miss?"

I shook my head, and he went away, leaving me convulsed. Oh, Scotland, I love you! A hundred bucks' worth of silk, the time of two women who'd already plenty to do, and a custom-made copy of a Paris original. But Andrew said we'd wait to see how it turned out.

The typewriter was still in my room when I went up for the cameras. It would go back to the record room as soon as someone had time. So I decided to make use of it while I could. I squandered sheets of guest notepaper, detailing the record room story for Aunt Agnes. I packed up the letter, took my equipment and spent three happy hours photographing house and garden before driving down to the post office. I was back well before teatime. The typewriter was gone from my room, and nobody was around when I came down dressed for sociability. Write a proper letter to my family for a change? The record room was empty. I found paper in the supply cabinet and was just finishing the letter when the door opened. "Who's here?" David's voice. . . .

"Sable."

He came around the file cabinets, his face grim. "What are you doing here? How did you get in?" he demanded harshly. "You were supposed to be finished—how long have you been here alone?"

There was something ugly, frightening, in his expression. "I am finished with the cards. The room was open, I was only writing my parents," I faltered. "I didn't realize you wouldn't wish the machine used, David. Sholto seemed not to mind yesterday."

"No, no, it's not that." He pulled himself together with an effort. "You don't understand, Sable. It's the insurance—uh, the premium's prohibitive, they didn't want to write a policy in the first place because the house isn't fireproof, so it's a basic condition that no one shall use the records unless I'm present." He ran his hand through his hair, smiling at me thinly. "Sorry I

112

barked at you, my dear, but they'd take any excuse to cancel. Makes me a bit twitchy."

I bet! "Why didn't you tell me? Of all people, I'd have understood—but I was only filling time before tea, didn't even have a cigarette." I pulled the letter from the machine. "I'll write out an envelope later."

"Well, well, no harm done," he said bluffly. "If you're ready, Sable? I admit I'd like to freshen before tea. . . ." We went out to the hall, and David firmly locked the record room behind me.

Of course he didn't know it was a barn door, from which the horse had already departed—via airmail to Aunt Agnes.

While I washed my hands in the powder room, I thought about the Laird's ugly snarl when he found me in the record room—and the insurance story. That be damned for a tall tale, I thought scornfully. I could admire his quick thinking, but he was still underestimating cousin Sable.

He'd be in a major flap when he found I hadn't gone to Aberdeen! Drying my hands a bit tremulously, I concocted a story. Because if I hadn't gone to Aberdeen, what *had* I been doing all day?

A good question—and the first David asked when Annis innocently inquired whether Nellie had found a suitable style for the silk. Even Sholto looked startled. His teacup suspended halfway to his mouth, he asked, "I thought you were buying a dress?"

I shook my head placidly. "Annis remembered some silk she had laid away—the wrong color for her, but perfect for me. I spent the morning consulting with Nellie and being measured—and wrote all the letters I should have written weeks ago." I smiled at David.

113

"The typewriter was in my room, to make notes for the Women's Institute."

"Annis persuaded Sable to address the Institute," Sholto told David. "Ye'll talk about your library, cousin?"

"Yes . . . but I'm not sure what to tell. I've twenty pages of notes." I looked hopefully at the Laird. "Would you have a moment to glance over them and say which?" Had I pulled it off? Not quite. . . .

"Delighted to help—but surely you didn't spend all day indoors over a typewriter? Annis, how could you interfere with Sable's vacation?"

"I didn't. I never meant. . . ." Annis said defensively. "Only because the hog man from Cheshire failed after it was too late to cancel the meeting, David. I thought Sable might say a few words about America or something."

I was pinch-hitting for a *hog man?* The absurdity was so delicious, it could only be played straight. "Now, don't fuss, David," I rebuked him, authoritatively. "Even a few words from the Laird's cousin must be absolutely right. Of course it didn't take all day. I photographed the outside of the house and the gardens." I eyed Sholto mischievously. "You said I mustn't go anywhere without your approval, cousin, but I couldn't believe there'd be vermin traps in the flower garden."

He laughed absently. "No, it's quite safe. So, ye'd no one to entertain ye all day? Very dull! Had I known I'd not have gone to Comynhaugh, but I thought ye were in Aberdeen."

"Rest easy, cousin. Your wishes were better obeyed here than there. Green it is, and if Nellie has her way,

114

it'll cling to the point she'll have to sew me into it like a film star."

Annis looked uneasy. "Not really so extreme, Sable? Nellie's very clever, but her taste isn't always suited for conservative society."

"Don't worry," I said penitently. "I think it's Balenciaga—but I couldn't resist needling our road company Diamond Jim Brady."

The Laird was still not deflected. "Then you did get some fresh air, Sable?"

"All afternoon," I assured him, "and if you'll forgive bluntness, I think I've got at least one, perhaps two shots of Strathmuir to use for guest cards when you're rid of these."

"That would be a relief," Annis remarked unexpectedly. "I never liked this one at all. When will your pictures be ready? I'm anxious to see them."

"Some should arrive before I leave—I put a special order on everything. They'll hold negatives and send a complete set of prints to you, David. If there's a picture you don't like, I'll destroy the negative."

Why didn't I add that a full set of prints was also being sent, as they were developed, directly to Aunt Agnes? For the same reason that I'd never told him she'd met his mother or that she had the wedding picture. Unconsciously I was now as wary as he, though I didn't know why.

At first, I'd wanted to protect Aunt Agnes from annoyance. Now I wanted protection for myself—but from what? We'd come around full circle: I hadn't liked these people at first sight, they hadn't liked me, and despite surface courtesy, the status was still quo . . . with one small difference. I know knew more of these people than they did of me.

Stupid humorless Annis loved her husband. Sholto was a temperish misanthrope, yet devoted to Clan lands. He'd been contemptuous when I described Aunt Agnes's wealth; I thought that was understandable. He didn't know I knew nothing of the succession. I'd been frightened of his anger on the fortalice, but Sholto's temper was quick and quickly over.

The Laird was another matter. He'd nearly convinced me of sincere dedication to Clan business. He was still an oily conniver and no gentleman. To my original dislike of his limited mind was added distrust for a sneak who'd steam open a letter—and finally, fear.

He was leaning back, relaxed, all suspicion apparently allayed, drinking tea and nibbling a cucumber sandwich while Sholto reported some estate matter. I picked up a square of sponge cake, and David's eyes flicked instantly to the tiny motion. . . .

As I ate the sponge cake and studied the sharp profile, I could no longer pretend that the thought, imbedded in my brain like a tiny splinter, was not there: This man, it persisted, was capable of killing. . . .

Chapter 8

For once, Sholto was absent from the dinner table. "He's gone to the MacLintock's," Annis said. "Was yours a successful trip, David?"

"Very! The mills can pay an extra dividend," he said expansively. "Afraid it changes plans a bit. I've asked the Earl of Camber and his wife for the twelfth."

"David, you didn't!"

"I did and he accepted." He glanced at her uneasily. "He backed my vote; how could I do less when he hinted rather broadly?"

Annis looked ready to faint. "She's second cousin to Her Majesty! Oh, David, how could you!"

"I didn't know Lady Camber was royalty," he muttered.

"What of it?" I inserted calmly. "Send up the typewriter to the morning room, David, with plenty of paper, pads, pencils, erasers, an extra ribbon and Burke's Peerage." Annis was staring hopelessly into space obviously on the verge of hysterics. "Is there a plan of the bedrooms?"

"Yes." David's thin lips tightened. He pushed away from the table. Standing up, he flung his napkin across the plate. I kept my eyes on the spreading gravy stain while he said viciously, "I'd no idea a simple invitation would create chaos. If you'll excuse me, I'll finish my dinner later."

After he stalked out of the room, I said, "No time for tears, Annis darling. Finish your dinner, then we'll retire to arrange."

"Yes. He's only overtired from travelling—I shouldn't have said anything," she murmured pathetically, "but royalty, Sable—it is difficult."

"I expect so, but we'll cope, never fear. I'm good for hours." And I was, if only to flummox David Kirby-Gordon who could make a nasty scene after having thrown a major problem at his wife.

By dinner's end, I knew Annis had had it. Instinctively I took over. "Go along, sweetie. Andrew, the Earl and Countess of Camber are coming for the twelfth. I'm going to help Lady Annis. Could we have coffee and brandy in her morning room, please?"

Andrew's eyes flickered; he knew the ramifications. "Aye. The machine's gone up already. I'll be within call o' the bell till ye're finished."

Annis was weeping softly when I got upstairs. I sent Nellie for aspirin and forced two cups of strong coffee and a large shot of brandy into my hostess. I studied the bedroom plan. It didn't seem particularly intricate to me. "I give up my room to the Earl, the Countess is next door; everything else stays as is, unless the Campbells accept, in which case they go across from the Cambers and we shift the Hampton-Smiths next to Sholto—and let them share a bath for two nights. It should be worth

118

it, to be at the same houseparty with an earl!"

"Yes, you've arranged it very cleverly," she said, anxiously scanning the plan, "but what about yourself?"

"A folding cot in here. Would you mind terribly sharing your bath for two nights, Annis?"

She shook her head, staring incredulously at the sheet. "How quickly you did it, Sable! Could you type the list for Andrew while I start the seating."

"Aside from titles, who's important?" I asked, scribbling names and sticking cards into the slots of the dinner plan "Lady Camber on David's right, Lady Jean to his left; the Earl to your right, Lord Everard to your left . . . Sholto next the Countess, the wittiest man next Lady Jean, the prettiest wives next Lord Everard and Lord Camber—and there you are."

"You make it sound simple, but some people are more important to David than others."

"Don't you know which?"

She shook her head dismally.

"I need more cigarettes," I said. "Back in a moment." Picking up the guest list, I sailed downstairs and sure enough, the record room was lighted.

David was leaning back in the desk chair, telephone to ear, looking fatuous. Talking to his mistress, I thought coldly, and retreated to create a clatter of heels in the hall. When I reopened the door, the phone was cradled and David's face was ugly. "Yes? Now what d'you want?"

"Annis needs the order of importance among your untitled guests." I stalked across and thrust the paper before him.

"Good God, can't she settle anything herself?"

"Of course. I can, too," I assured him coldly, "by putting Mrs. Exeter beside the Earl and Mrs. Marsh next Lord Everard. It occurred to us, however, that for business reasons you might have a preference for these honored seats. But if it's immaterial," I swept up the list, "so much the better."

He snatched the paper violently. "Damn, of course it makes a difference."

"So I thought," I grinned.

He laughed reluctantly, swiftly numbering names. "Where'd you learn so much?"

"At mother's knee, where else?" I said lightly, reaching for the paper. He held onto it as he reached to replenish his brandy glass and tossed off the shot in one gulp. I suddenly realized he was drunk, though holding it well.

"Never learned anything from my mother, she was only a chambermaid."

"So what?" I murmured uncomfortably. "I'll take this back to Annis, shall I? Sorry I disturbed you, David."

"Don't run away, sit down—have a drink with me, eh?" He fumbled for a glass in the cabinet behind him, his hand still pressed on the list. Then he turned back to fill both glasses unsteadily.

"Not tonight, please? Annis is waiting." He had removed his hand from the list, but caught my wrist when I reached for it.

"Let 'er wait," he grunted, tugging me to the chair. I sat and accepted the brandy while he downed another. "My mother was a good woman. She did her best, but she'd nothing to give me. I'd all to do for myself," he muttered, gripping my hand.

120

"I'm sure she loved you dearly, David."

"She must have done, to endure me." He refilled his glass and released my hand, drawing a wallet from his breast pocket. "W'd you like to see 'er picture?"

"Of course," I said politely, but before I could twitch the list away, he'd set his elbow on it, bracing himself to open the wallet and turning a faded snapshot toward me. I glanced at it—and suppressed a gasp. I was looking at the face of a totally strange woman!

Instinctively I leaned forward for a second look. Facial planes and bone structure can't alter completely with age. I was staring at a gaunt, thin-faced woman, narrow-boned, with light eyes and sparse light hair that was probably sandy gray. No question that this was David's mother, the likeness was startling . . . but Mary Kirby had been small and cuddlesome, with wavy hair, full pouting lips. Even after twenty years of adversity, she could never have looked like this.

He withdrew it to gaze at it sentimentally, while I sat whirling in bewilderment. Could Aunt Agnes have shown me the wrong picture? I remembered those efficient files, her instant identification when the picture fell to the floor. And she'd *met* Mary Kirby. It was no mistake, I'd seen Mary Kirby's picture and she was *not* the woman in his snapshot. Then who was she?

Or—who was he?

"Only picture I 'ave, poor old mum. If she'd lived, I'd 'ave made things easier for 'er," he sighed. I felt frozen in sheer terror. I dared not let him suspect that I saw anything wrong. He might have been maudlin enough to show me the picture, but he hadn't built the Clan business by missing a trick or boozing himself under a table.

"You're . . . very like her, David."

"Yes," he said thickly. "She was right pretty when she was young. She had to work too hard, and I was trouble to her. I meant to make it up, but when I had the chance, it was too late."

"If that's your only picture, wouldn't you like me to copy it?"

"I don't want to give it up. If it's lost, I'll have nothing."

"I could do it here, before your eyes," I said persuasively. "Do let me, David! I've been at a loss to repay your hospitality—but here's a tiny something you'd like, and the easiest thing in the world for me."

He focused his eyes deliberately, and his lips slowly curved into a sly conspiratorial smile. "Here? Even developing and printing, so I can watch?" I nodded, too concentrated on getting a copy of that picture to be on guard. "Eh, you're a little love, Sable!" He lunged forward and captured my hand again. "We'll drink to it!" He refilled the glasses lavishly, squeezing my hand and chuckling. "Here's to my American sweetheart."

Well, you don't argue with a drunk. David's fingers were a steel grip. "I can't drink to myself," I protested, gaily raising my glass. "Here's to the Laird o'Gordon!" I got it down somehow. Then, with a smile— deliberately, dashingly, I tossed the glass over my shoulder to crash against a file cabinet. I'd a desperate hope the sound might startle him into relaxing his grasp.

It didn't work. He threw himself back in his chair with a falsetto titter, but his hand only dragged me with him. "C'me here, w'll seal it with a kiss. Aaah, you're a pretty thing, c'me here, luv. . . ."

122

He'd pulled me half across the desk. Now he was moving his hand sideways trying to get me around beside him. I was utterly petrified by his strength. "David, no! Oh, aren't you the naughty man," I giggled, trying to pull free. "I only came for a tiny decision, and you've made me tiddly. Shame on you, you wicked creature! Do let me go . . . time enough for a kiss when I've copied the picture." It was beginning to work. His fingers were loosening as he chortled at my coyness.

I'd nearly made it—and the hall door opened. "David?" Sholto stood in the doorway. His expression was dreadful; John Knox could not have been more revolted. "I beg your pardon, thought you were alone."

"Sholto, come and have a drink," I cried wildly. "David, get another glass?" I was still stretched nearly full-length over the desk, David's hand slackening. I pleaded silently over my shoulder, and Sholto came forward easily.

"A drink is it? I'll not say no."

"Good boy," David mumbled, looking about vaguely. "Where're the glasses? Oh, I remember—you broke yours, Sable. Eh, you're a jolly little luv!" He chuckled and hiccuped faintly, but at last my hand was free. "Watch out for the splinters—first time a girl ever broke a glass for me," he tittered, nearly falling as he swung back to the cabinet. "No matter, we've more. We've more of everything these days, eh, Sholto?"

"That we have," Sholto agreed, staring at me coldly, "and too much of some things. I'm sorry to interrupt."

"You didn't. I only came for David's decision on dinner seating." Before the Laird had negotiated the return to his desk, I seized the list and fled. "Thanks for the drink, good night. . . ."

Annis looked up from the menus. "You've been an age, what happened to you? Were you ill?"

"No, I was in the record room getting David to mark the order of importance. Now we'll be done in a minute."

"You—went into the record room?" Her voice was a mere whisper, her face ghost-white. So she knew what I'd found.

"Yes. He gave me a glass of brandy, numbered the names. . . . Sholto came in, I came out, and here I am," I said, briskly checking the table plan. "And there we are! You were only out by one: the Hampton-Smiths are more important than Exeters, so they go next to Sholto. How are you coming with the menus?"

She was still pallid, but breathing more easily. "I don't know, I can't seem to think."

"Would you like to leave it to me, Annis?" I asked after a moment. "Sometimes it's easier just to check or change completed lists. . . ."

"Could you? I'm so tired, Sable."

"Of course. To bed and forget it!" I walked her across the corridor to her room.

Nellie came forward from the dressing room, her eyes widening at Annis's drooping figure. "Och, it's bed ye need, milady. Come awa' wi' me," Nellie said, "and we'll have ye tucked up snug in a minute."

I went back to the morning room, doused most of the lights, and eyed the guest list marked by Lord David Kirby-Gordon. Very delicately I picked it up by one corner and reconnoitered, but Strathmuir seemed silent. I scuttled around to my room, dropped the paper on the edge of my bed. It contained, I knew, two sets of fingerprints only: mine—and the Laird's.

By hook or crook, it was going special post to Scotland Yard.

The night wasn't over. I transferred the typewriter to my room, made a final trip for supplies, and locked my door. Wearily, I undressed and settled before the tiny coal fire. Now it was time to think, and I was instantly aware that I'd really known all along. . . .

The Laird was not David Kirby.

He was *not* a forty-six-year-old man who'd never been out of England aside from the Anzio landing. He had not spent months learning to use his left hand. This was a left-handed English man who was at least fifty-five and well acquainted with America. By all odds and despite recessive genes, he ought to be brown-eyed and mesomorphic but was instead a fine-boned ectomorph. I lit a cigarette—and remembered his words about English versus American tobacco blends.

Wherever he came from, whoever he was, this man knew America. He was acquainted with maple syrup, lemon instead of milk for tea, and scrapple. Only someone who had visited Philadelphia would know scrapple; even in America, nobody else eats the stuff.

And he'd identified my name, known there was a Cape Sable in Nova Scotia. It made a faint pattern. Not Liverpool, I thought, but someplace nearby, from which he'd drifted to the docks and shipped out on the Atlantic run . . . for all the things he knew were American East Coast. If he really had been a Liverpool water rat, he would never have risked recognition going to board meetings in that city.

That was why he wouldn't go abroad on vacation, permitted no publicity pictures; he couldn't chance identification of a business photograph. It was also why he'd never had his mother's picture copied.

I had thought him capable of murder. Now I had a *reason,* and with a shiver, I was on my feet pacing back and forth. Inexplicable, incredible that he could have avoided detection for twenty years! Was I merely an hysterical woman? Could there be any other explanation? My suspicion rested on a faded photograph, seen in dim light when I'd had a stiff brandy.

No, I wasn't wrong; that was David's mother, and she was not the woman Aunt Agnes had met.

There couldn't be anything in the record room; he'd long since have destroyed it. Yet he didn't want me to use the files unsupervised. He'd been relieved that my dates were 1860 forward, which had led me to go backward. I was still certain that I'd hit it, that there was more significance to the extra child than I knew. He could never have merely deleted from those files. It would have required a major job of re-indexing and left a noticeable gap. Too many people knew about the gypsy. Aunt Agnes had said the Laird seemed anxious to forget Romany blood. . . . No doubt—because he hadn't any. Then who was he? How had he worked the imposture; known enough to assume the Laird's name? Could he have known the real David Kirby extremely well. . . . Could he have been a Gordon by-blow left over from the first war, not legally entitled to succession but filling a dead boy's shoes? Death duties again—if only I knew more British law.

Annis didn't know, I thought suddenly; she'd been innocently surprised at his knowledge of America. Did Sholto know? Fantastic, but odd things do happen through wars. Imagine a dead David, a reportedly dead Sholto, and the illegitimate relative taking over—only to learn that Sholto was alive. To confess would have ruined a nearly bankrupt estate. I'd buy that, I decided. Sholto, already landed and titled, might have kept silent, knowing the entail would automatically get back to the proper heirs, since David had no son.

That would explain why Sholto lived here, managed the land . . . and wished me gone. He was smart enough to know I was potentially dangerous. Sholto knew I had brains, while the Laird knew only one sort of woman: the jolly little luv. . . .

I thought of David's snapshot again. . . . I was willing to bet that woman was Welsh by her bone structure. Wales isn't far from Liverpool. . . . I thought of George Kirby, who might or might not be descended from the wedlock son of the first David Kirby, but was certainly a Romany devil for looks . . . and old enough to get a son before the first war.

Was *that* it? Was David a by-blow of George Kirby, older than the real David, but perhaps knowing of him, even growing up together in Liverpool or nearby? I could buy that, too; David *looked* nothing like George Kirby, but there was a sort of panache in his business dealings that could easily be the heritage of a Rom.

Gradually, I grew more calm as I thought it through—but there remained the question of what to do? I didn't want to upset the applecart heedlessly, perhaps create scandal—or destroy everything the Laird had worked twenty years to achieve. For a few minutes I wondered what good would it do for me to know, after all? Why not burn the list and forget it?

I couldn't do it. It would require the utmost caution, but I had to be sure. "Dear John, on the typed list you will find two sets of prints; one is mine. I have put a full set for checking on the blank page. Please try to identify the others through the War Office and let Lord Everard know what you find. However, he is not under any circumstances to tell me publicly! He is probably coming here for the grouse shoot; there's a big party in my honor."

I pressed my fingers on a sheet of notepaper and addressed an envelope. Suddenly recalling the Laird's ugly face in the record room, I added a postscript. "Please hurry, John. I'm scared."

I delicately folded the fingerprinted list into the envelope. I would stick the letter under my pillow and set the alarm for 7:30. This letter must catch the first post from Strathbogie.

I was ready to fall into bed when there was a tap at the door. I stood frozen, knowing I'd locked it but half-expecting. . . .

Another tap. "Sable—cousin, ye're awake?" Sholto asked.

I stole to the door. "Yes?"

"Open to me, cousin."

Hesitantly, I turned the key and opened the door an inch, but he made no move. He was still in dinner jacket over the bright plaid kilt, "He didna fright ye?"

I shook my head. "Not the first time I've met a man who'd had a few after a good day's work."

Sholto's hands unclenched slowly. "It's the devil I'd be away, but how could I know ye'd be rambling about to encounter him." He drew a deep breath. "Please, cousin—keep yourself to yourself till we're through this party. Stay with Annis, photograph the mill, sew the seams of your dress, make your speech—what ye will, but stay away from the record room and David. Understand?"

Chapter 9

The alarm woke me. I was up and dressed in five minutes. The letter was securely buttoned under my blouse when I unlocked the door and listened. All was silent except a faraway sound from the servants' wing. I trotted swiftly downstairs and slipped through the garden. I had my cameras along for an alibi. Luck was with me until the last moment. I had the car in low gear and was headed out the driveway when Sholto emerged from a side path. He stopped briefly at the sight of me, then sprang forward. "Where are you going?"

"Morning photographs," I called gaily, waving my hand and accelerating dangerously. I made the curve and was gone before he could reach the car. In the rear view mirror, I could see him glaring after me. Then I was around the privet and rolling down to the high road, my hands trembling on the steering wheel— driving with all possible speed for Strathbogie. I was afraid he'd come in pursuit, but I reached the town with no sign of him.

The square was slumberous, yawning awake for the

day to come. The post office had just opened. I bought air-special stamps and slid the letter into the slot with a shiver of relief. It was done. The only threat now was the postal clerk. If he realized that the letter deposited by the Laird's cousin was directed to Scotland Yard. . . . A calculated risk, I decided, going back for the cameras. Strathbogie might learn, but it was unlikely it'd filter back to Strathmuir at once. I had a hunch the town wasn't on intimate terms with the Marquess of Huntly.

There were peculiar stones in the center of Strathbogie that I had been wanting to photograph since my arrival. Nobody knew anything about them, but they had to be Druidic, like Stonehenge. They were beautiful in their weathered dignity. When I focused from one side, pedestrians going to work politely crossed to walk behind me; when I changed angles, so did the people. A few lingered politely. A cocky youngster said, "Ye'll no' get the full range till ye go up t'clock tower, mistress."

I looked at the thing and was as dizzying as the fortalice. "Thank you very much. . . ."

"Miss Lennox, ye're early abroad." Bess MacDanald smiled at me, market basket on one arm. "Come awa' in, do, for a cup."

Nearly ten before I drove into the courtyard. Sholto was waiting for me. He clenched my shoulders and shook me like a rag doll. "Whaur hae ye been so lang?" he demanded harshly. "Whyfor d'ye go dashing off at crack o'dawn?"

"Please, I only went to photograph the stones," I quavered. "And I had a cup of tea with Mrs. MacDanald."

"Why could ye no' tell me afore ye left? Ye saw me, dinna deny it!"

His fury aroused mine. "I wasn't aware you were my keeper, or that I should report to you before taking out my own car to drive the public roads."

"If I were your keeper, ye wouldna be here," he returned, "but whether I will or no, I'm responsible for ye. I thought I'd been explicit enough; do ye customarily disregard instructions?" Under his implacable gaze, I hung my head. "If not too troublesome, I'd appreciate knowing what ye have in mind for the rest of this day," he said, with insulting courtesy. "I've tasks of my own, ye understand, already two hours behind. Shall I cancel the rest, to be at your disposal?"

I swallowed hard. No point in fighting, things were difficult enough. "Please, I never meant to disrupt your plans, Sholto. I'll stay here the rest of the day," I said.

"Hmph," he snorted, "and the instant I take my eye of ye, ye'll be just stepping out for your damned pictures, or poking your nose somewhere it doesna belong."

"I promise. I'll even stay in the house if you like."

He was not mollified. "Do that," he stated, "preferably in your own room, until I get back to look after you." He gave a short whistle that brought Jennie trotting around the barn, and strode off toward the jeep.

Late as it was, the breakfast room was still fully equipped, awaiting me, which only added to my nervousness. I'd not only upset Sholto, now the staff would be annoyed. "I'm so sorry, Andrew . . . I only want toast and coffee. I could even take it upstairs if it'd be easier. . . ."

"The way ye'll leave crumbs all over your room, inviting the mice to sleep wi' ye," he said severely. "Ye'll eat your breakfast like a gentlewoman, and when you're finished," he waggled his eyebrows austerely, "ye'll go along to the workroom for a fitting, the way Nellie can put her mind to her work." Then he chuckled kindly. "Take your time, mistress. All's left in case the Laird should fancy elevens—forbye, he's gone to Inverness, but we dinna change the routine; 'tis easier to be systematic."

David away? That was a relief. "Where's Lady Annis?"

"Working over the arrangements," he said. "She did say she'd give us lists for rooms and seating, miss."

"Yes. Leave the machine in my room. Andrew . . ."

"Yes, Miss Lennox?"

"Would it be unduly officious of me to—take over?"

"It'd be a dom' fine thing did ye get anything settled, the way we'd know how to go on," he said flatly. There was a long silence while I finished my coffee. "Ye'll go along to Nellie first," he said. "Mrs. Frame'll be waiting with me, afterwards. . . ."

Going upstairs, I was obeying Sholto's orders but still meddling. What would he disapprove of now? "Annis, may I come in?"

"Of course, Sable." She was alarmingly pale, frantic. "I'm afraid I'm being a very bad hostess, but you do understand?"

"Yes." I gently removed her scribbled, scratched-out pads and set my sheaf of notes before her. "Here are the menus. Could you just glance over them to see if there's anything glaringly wrong?"

Silently she studied the sheets until her lips twisted. "Will you cope, Sable?" she looked at me defenselessly. "It's not fair to ask, but there's so little time and I'm—slow-witted."

"Not really. You're simply one of those people who can't function under pressure—which doesn't mean the adrenalin kids who rise to a challenge do better in the end," I told her soberly. "Anyway, after twenty years David should know better."

"It's my duty, I ought to be able to plan," she sighed.

"You know you can't, and after twenty years, the staff knows it too," I said gently. "It upsets them to watch you struggle, when they are so willing to do it for you. Be content to be what you are. Do the things you know you do well, delegate the rest—and the hell with what David expects." I shuffled the notes together and smiled at her. "Hadn't you better be thinking what you mean to wear?"

That was the day. At luncheon: "The Lady Annis has gone to the garden club meeting, saying all ye decide meets her approval."

"I see, Andrew. You'll prevent any serious American error?"

"Ye'll make none, ye were born knowing," Andrew said calmly.

Typing, consultations, second thoughts, retyping—by midafternoon the job was complete, including a time schedule for Mrs. Frame to fit preparation into normal routine. Only details remained: flowers, garage space, place cards and such. Andrew produced a dusty box. "The Lady Margaret hand-wrote the menu," he

135

observed. "Her script was much admired." Wrapped in tissue, the gilt-edged cards were still flat and fresh. I could do them . . . but twenty?

Or would there be twenty? Andrew knew only that there was a letter from Cascadine in the mail awaiting the Laird. "Place a call for me, please?" I got Lady Jean and chatted casually until the extension was replaced, then I said urgently, "I can't explain, but you must come. I need you."

She was silent for an agonizing moment. "'Tis serious or ye wouldna call," she reflected. "Aye, we'll come, but we'd written to decline. How will ye explain?"

"What reason did you give?"

"The truth: we're bespoke for the Duke of Cargill."

"How can you cancel him?"

She chuckled. "Verra easily, he's m'brother—a standing invitation. But do I tell him we're asked to honor Agnes Ware's grand-niece, he'll cancel his shoot to meet ye."

"How many miles away? How large a party?"

"Thirty or forty miles, probably no more than ten— what had ye in mind, child?"

"Would he bring them here for the buffet dinner and dance on Thursday? Then I could say he's released you, in return for the chance to meet a relative of Agnes Ware."

"It is verra serious," she said. "Are ye sure ye'd rather not come away to us at once?"

"No, because I might be wrong."

"Alex'll bring his party to Strathmuir," she promised quietly. "I shall have to say ye're uneasy, and I don't know why, but it'd help did he lend his support." She

136

laughed. "He'll be there! He wouldna miss on a mystery, for all he doesna like the Laird overmuch. 'Tis a clever idea, Sable—but be careful, child!"

I went to find Andrew. "The Campbells are coming, and ten more for dinner Thursday—the Duke of Cargill is bringing his party." Andrew dropped the spoon he was polishing and stared at me. "I'll need India ink, water colors and fine brushes to attempt the place cards."

"I've the Lady Margaret's materials put by, if they're usable."

They were. I culled from flower and kitchen garden, while Sandy drove to town for fresh ink and more brushes. Three cards were embellished when Nellie came in to request a fitting. Andrew arrived as she departed. "Sandy's returned, mistress—and also the Laird. 'Tis early tea," he warned, "the way ye'll be on time for the Institute, with dinner afterwards."

Heavens, I'd forgotten my maiden speech! Bending over the cards, I put the finishing touch on a fourth. "Just this one, Andrew . . . will it do?"

He peered over my shoulder. "Och, aye," he approved, pursing his lips. "Did ye put the name of each guest at the top, we'd no' need place cards."

Out of shower, and rushing into my clothes and makeup, I concentrated on the Laird: what sort of drunk was he, would he remember last night?

He probably held his liquor by his ears, with total recall and no hangovers. It had to be so, or in twenty years there'd have been gossip. He drank in the record room; Sholto and Annis knew it. Now I knew it, too. Would David make any sort of pitch about it . . . or ignore it, on the assumption I was a jolly little luv, good for fun and games?

I knew this was a crucial meeting, the first after last night. Had he decided how to play it, or was he going to play it by ear, based on what I did or said?

I had three good smokescreens: the Campbell acceptance, the speech, and the coup of acquiring the Duke of Cargill. One or another should red-herring any awkward question . . . but walking into the salon, I knew at a glance all resources were needed.

David was pinch-lipped and unsmiling. Annis was pale and looking at her hands, and there was a reckless tilt to Sholto's head.

"I'm sorry to be late, and perhaps you'll wish I hadn't come at all, David," I apologized, wide-eyed and wistful, "because I seem to have invited the Duke of Cargill and his guests to your dance. Sholto—no tea today, fix me a drink for love o' the Gordons?"

"The Duke of Cargill?" David echoed, stunned.

"I didn't know what else to *do,* David, when Lady Jean said he'd released them on condition he could meet Agnes Ware's relative."

Sholto produced the highball. "Begin at the beginning, cousin," he suggested. "Here's David with a refusal from Lord Everard, but now ye say they're coming after all?"

"The duke remembers Aunt Agnes. The instant he heard I was here and the Campbells invited but not himself, Lady Jean was on the phone. I wasn't sure you'd permit it—but since you had wanted them in the first place, I thought you'd surely still want them—and what's ten more for a buffet, after all?"

David found his voice. "Of course, of course, he's more than welcome—but where were you, Annis? Why

138

was Sable alone?"

Was he wondering if I'd got into the records again? "I sent her to the garden club," I said placidly. "Nellie fitted my dress, and in between I've been typing Annis's arrangements for the party." I took a long swallow of the drink and remembered that the best defense is a good offense. "I must say, David, you're extremely thoughtless! You'd never expect this amount of detail work in so short a time from any employee—and Annis doesn't even type.

"If I'd known your hospitality for me would mean so much work for Annis, I'd have told you to send her your private secretary for two days," I said severely— and guessed by his glazed eyes and blank face that the secretary was the mistress. Did Annis know? I didn't look at her, but swept on. "I don't know why she already hasn't a girl to handle correspondence and club notes. You could perfectly well afford it, David, for the sake of your wife's prestige, if nothing else."

The Laird was flushed an ugly mottled red. "I've no doubt matters are better arranged in America, but hereabouts," he sneered, "it's assumed that a titled lady is capable of doing the work required for her 'prestige,' as you put it."

I finished my drink and extended the glass to Sholto, who silently took it away and refilled. "Not her prestige. Yours," I said softly. "Darling David, if you want a fight, you'll get one! You're a titled gentleman; you have secretaries to handle details, why should your wife have less? You expect her to represent her position suitably, to chair and secretary for local community projects, manage Strathmuir—and spend half the night writing her notes? Or should she take a typing

139

course?" He'd gone from red to ashen, and the room was still. I continued: "My Laird you may be, and honoring me extravagantly, but Annis is my Lady, and if she's too gentle to speak for herself, I'll do it for her. If Lady Jean has a girl twice a week, why not Lady Annis?"

David fingered his chin nervously, as Sholto put a highball in my hand. "If you needed help why the devil didn't you tell me?" he whirled on Annis, but for once she had an answer.

"You wouldn't have believed me."

Touch and go for a minute, but I caught David's eye and grinned wickedly, until he capitulated. "All right, get someone, then." He was still inclined to snipe. "Better yet, let Sable hire a girl. No doubt she'll know better than you."

I faced him squarely. "Was I too rude? Shall we call the whole thing off, and I'll leave with apologies for sticking my nose where it 'doesna belong'?"

"No, of course not, Sable," he said impatiently, and fixed a drink for himself. Then with a dry laugh, "I meant it: hire a girl for Annis—and before you go, come to Liverpool and tell me what's wrong there!"

At seven o'clock I stood in the community hall, being introduced by Annis as "our cousin from overseas, Miss Sable Gordon-Lennox, who is in charge of a photographic library in New York and who has kindly consented to tell us something of her work. Ladies and gentlemen, Miss Gordon-Lennox." This was evidently one of the things Annis could do without a quiver, while I felt a disastrous lack of adrenalin.

140

For one thing, I'd understood there was to be only a small group of women, but the hall was crowded to the point of standees, with an unexpected proportion of men. I could see Ranald MacDanald, and—far to the rear, leaning against the wall with folded arms— Sholto. Had the Laird come, too?

"Ladies and gentlemen," I said shakily, "I must ask your indulgence. I've never made a speech before—at least, not in public. . . ." It was easier than I'd thought; these people had come prepared to like me. I explained my routine work briefly, and by the time I'd finished the first anecdote, I sensed the audience was wholly with me. It was an exhilarating experience! They laughed heartily when a story was funny; they were soberly intent at serious moments, even applauded the Dahomey-UNICEF coup, and literally guffawed at the predicament of the young engineer who wound up owning a slave in Tunisia because he didn't believe in slavery—after he'd bought her, he'd found he couldn't set her free!

I hadn't meant to tell that one, but the audience was so receptive. I threw it in for the finale. We were through exactly at eight. While I shook hands with various people, I had a glimpse of Sholto disappearing, carrying a small suitcase. There was no sign of him when Annis firmly moved us away from the crowd. This was apparently another thing she was good at; somehow we were away, without giving offense. Driving back to Strathmuir, she was (for Annis) positively animated! "I've never seen the hall so well filled! We always hope the women will bring their husbands for evening meetings, but as Lady Atherton said, this was a subject to interest men. She was very pleased with you, Sable."

"I'm glad I did a creditable job."

"My dear, it was a triumph! A pity David wasn't there—he never will come, and it's such a shame he should have missed . . ."

But he hadn't missed it. Sholto had borrowed the tape recording privately commissioned by Ranald MacDanald!

"He'll never miss the chance for publicity, the way he'll sell more film," Sholto grinned, "but all to the good. After dinner you'll hear our cousin distinguishing herself, David."

I'd tried to excuse myself to finish the place menus; David wouldn't hear of it, nor was Annis any help. "I'd rather like to hear it again, Sable; one misses a lot on the stage, behind a speaker."

"One misses a lot at the back when there's as much laughter as Sable produced. I'll hear it again myself." Sholto pressed the button, and there I was. On the whole, though, it was a good way to fill the evening: no chance of conversation or any slip that might alarm the Laird.

David made a definite dent in the brandy bottle, but was entirely, sharply, attentive to the end. Sholto was not. Around eleven-thirty, Andrew hovered in the doorway. "Lord Aboyne, 'tis Jennie." Sholto was on his feet at once. "Ye'll forgive me, cousin?"

"O'course. Am I no' female, too, the way a man is a comfort at such moments?"

Sholto laughed, striding to the door. "Ye're too understanding, cousin. . . ."

By midnight, when I switched off the recorder, David was bosky, but still capable of loud approval.

142

Needless to say the story he'd liked best was the boy stuck with a slave girl! "Well, I'm glad you're pleased, David." I stifled a yawn. "Annis, I'm for bed, how about you?"

David sat relaxed as we got to our feet. "You're deserting me," he complained.

"Not forever darling." I blew him a kiss and drew Annis with me toward the door. "Your harem is tired. See you tomorrow."

"Harem? Eh, that's a good one," he laughed uproariously, stretching out an aimless hand. "C'me here, give us a kiss good night."

I could feel Annis trembling beside me. "Not tonight, me laddie-buck," I crooned, thrusting her ahead of me and swiftly patting the Laird's head. "Ye wouldn't appreciate it." I'd withdrawn my hand before he could seize it. "Good night, milord, and sweet dreams of Annie Laurie."

Securely locked into my room, I undressed wearily. One day gone; with luck, I'd avoid the Laird until he was occupied with guests at tomorrow's tea. If my letter caught John Morrisy first post tomorrow, he'd have an answer to telephone Lord Everard before they left Cascadine . . . so I'd know if I were crazy or not when I sat for dinner.

As I came from the bathroom, I thought I heard pebbles on a window. Surreptitiously I peeked out and saw a lantern below. I jumped back at a second handful of gravel on the window. "Cousin, ye're awake?"

I pulled aside the draperies, threw open the window and leaned out. "Yes . . . what's the basket?"

143

"Three dogs and a bitch," Sholto said, softly joyous. "Mother and basket doing well. Will ye take one of the pups for your own, cousin?"

"That I will. A male for choice since ye've three." I'd give it to Aunt Agnes for the summer home. Looking down on the merry smiling face beneath the lantern, my heart turned over. He was too much man, too much a reminder. "Ye'll pat Jennie for me? Good night, cousin."

As I tumbled into bed and stared into the darkness, I told myself, "It's ridiculous—merely because of hands on a steering wheel, light on a face, a twinkle in the eye . . ." But for the first time in nearly eight years I cried myself to sleep. . . .

Chapter 10

The Laird emerged for breakfast with such promptness
that I knew he'd been lurking. He was wreathed in
jovial smiles, a happy little bundle of sunshine. What, I
wondered grimly, was in that sharp mind? It developed
that David knew *I* had called Lady Jean. I took the
wind out of his sails by admitting it at once. "I hope you
don't mind?" I said.

"Of course not, my dear—but why?"

"I had to know if they were coming," I said surprised,
"but wasn't it lucky? They weren't sure you'd let them
change their minds—and if you didn't, they'd be in
disgrace with the Duke! Well, I knew you couldn't have
received the letter, being gone all day—easy enough to
expand a buffet—I chanced you'd approve."

"Of course." He smiled, the crooked curve of the lips
was somehow sly. "It appears this is your party in more
ways than one."

"I did think it might be a tiny feather for the bonnet,"
I confided. "One marquess, two earls, why not a duke?"

David laughed. "Eh, you're clever! Well now—what

145

shall we do today, my dear? Photograph the mill, drive around the estate? There's a very pleasant stream if you care to fish. I'm at your disposal until the guests arrive."

Spend hours alone with this man? "Kind of you, but I've masses of things to do," I said rapidly, "final fittings, place cards, diary. . . ."

Before he could say anything, Sholto came through the pantry door. He stopped dead at sight of us. "Good morning all," he said, going over to pour a cup of tea. "What's afoot?"

"I was just telling David I've things to keep me busy. . . ."

"And I was about to tell Sable she's a guest, not a skivvy," David broke in smoothly. "She's not to be exhausted for her own party."

"No more she shall." Sholto spread an oatcake with jam and chomped with gusto. "I'm taking her to Comynhaugh. Why not come with us, David," he asked a bit thickly.

The Laird began to flush and his eyes narrowed meanly.

"Actually, David booked me first," I broke in, "but in any case, I do have chores for the morning."

Sholto nodded placidly, stuffing the rest of the oatcake in his mouth and happily licking his fingers. "Noon, then—and we'll choose the dogs ye want, David, while Sable takes her pictures. Then we'll come back the other way for a look at the blinds."

So it was only a trip Sholto had to make, and he'd thought to take me along for the ride. That was evidently David's interpretation, too, for he was good-humoured again . . . although why should he care if I were alone with Sholto? At least I couldn't be in the record room, I thought indignantly, and excused myself.

"Oh, are you going? See you later, cousin."

"Yes," I said sweetly. But it was going to be much later, I decided, after settling to work on the menu cards. Damned if I was going to be caught in the middle. Let Andrew tell them Miss Lennox was being fitted or something.

Ten minutes past noon. "Lord Aboyne is waiting," Andrew stated, "and ye'll no' make it if ye dinna start at once. The Lawsons have arrived already, 'tis fortunate the Laird was here. We'd no planned extra for luncheon, but do ye go with Lord Aboyne, we'll have enough—and Mrs. Frame asks will ye get all the flowers ye can from Comynhaugh?"

Why didn't I say I was too busy, I'd be happy with a sandwich? "I'll be down directly, Andrew."

The jeep stood in pale sunshine, no sign of driver. "Sholto?"

"Come choose your pup, cousin." Jennie lay in barn shadows, proudly surveying four staggering bundles of fluff. There was one tawny rascal. "I'll take him, he's a Gordon Red like myself."

"I knew you'd pick that one," Sholto chuckled, "but it's not a him, it's a her—and I warrant she'll be as much trouble as you."

I stood up, laughing helplessly. "Am I so very evil, then?"

"That ye are," he nodded, pushing me into the jeep. "The Kirk would never approve ye, cousin."

"And you don't, either," I sighed, "but I try to be good."

"A waste of time! With that red hair and quick tongue, ye'll never see Heaven," he teased; "forbye ye captivated the town last night."

"Lady Atherton was very pleased, and Annis said they'd never had so many men, but it was a subject to interest them," I said.

Sholto snorted wickedly. "You were the subject to interest them. Did ye not know the whole town turned out to get a good look at ye? The MacDanalds spread the word ye'd be worth hearing; you're already known by the hair, I told ye it was a sure passport—and atop all, the Laird is giving a sensational party in your honor! Who could resist taking a peek?" He laughed at my stunned expression. "Every detail of the menus, the lists, even the picture of your dress is known to everyone in town," he assured me. "It's agreed ye'll be the belle of the evening—I can scarce wait for the entrance myself." He laughed again. "My dear little cousin, it's a small town. Any visitor provides a welcome change, but you've set Strathbogie on its ears! Half the town's ordered this American coffee maker; Mrs. Frame's parcelled out your American recipes to a favored few; Nellie's reported your measurements to everyone . . . there's heartburn over that twenty-two inch waist, I shouldn't wonder!"

I was half-amused, half-appalled. "Oh, dear—will David like that?"

Sholto stopped laughing. He turned the jeep into a driveway. "What if he does or doesn't?" he asked harshly, braking before a pleasant country house. "Ye'll be gone in two days, cousin—or were ye planning

148

to stay forever?"

"You know I'm leaving with the Campbells—"

"Aye, but ye came for two days, ye're still here, so there might be other extensions." He swung out onto the gravelled path and went forward to throw open the door, while I crawled out. Why was he always so grim the instant I mentioned the Laird? I didn't want to think Sholto in league with an impostor, but what else could explain his reactions? It was sincere flattery, in a way: he didn't underestimate me, wanted me away from David who thought I was dumb.

Slowly, I picked up the cameras and turned. Sholto stood in the entrance beside an elderly beanpole of a woman. "Come along, Sable," he said impatiently. "Bessie, here's Miss Lennox. Take care of her, will you?" He vanished, while Bessie looked me up and down.

Finally, she broke into a broad smile. "A true Gordon," she said cordially, "and as pretty as they tell't me! Come awa' in, mistress. Ye'll like summat to eat, then we'll get the flowers." She led me to a sunny kitchen. "Ye'll no' object to informality," she asked, "sin' the Laird winna be here?"

"Of course not." But it was a shaky minute before I realized she didn't mean David. At Comynhaugh, Sholto was Laird. Either way, I was relieved to be alone.

I was more alone than I knew. When I'd finished in the gardens, a fresh-faced gawking lad appeared. "The Laird's detained in the byre, mistress. I'm to take ye back."

We went in a station wagon. Bessie firmly put me behind the driver, as befitted a lady. The flowers were tenderly piled about me, a selection of guns stared at me from the front seat—and six hunting dogs whuffled and slavered happily over my neck from the rear.

The Party had begun.

Motor cars, chockablock in the garage court, had Sandy perspiring over storage. I enlisted the lad from Comynhaugh to assist. "Ye'll trust him, Sandy, the way he's a careful man with a machine." That he was, returning me at twenty miles per hour and stating firmly that anything more was "excessive."

Nipping into the rear hall I saw Andrew, whose face cleared at sight of me. "Be quick to dress, the Laird has asked for ye—and I made bold to retrieve the menus."

Mrs. Frame bounced out, looking distracted. "The sandwiches are nearly gone, we've used the cake for tomorrow. 'Tis a bedlam, mistress, and the Laird calling for drinks, the way we're short of ice already."

"Send someone to beg the aid of the soda fountain—and Mrs. MacDanald," I said calmly. "Spread plain biscuits with cheese; broil and serve hot when the sandwiches run out."

"Aye, she'll manage." Andrew had forgotten all protocol, and was pushing me testily to the stairs. "Go along, do, lass!"

The guests had already subtly split between U and non-U. The peerage was drinking tea; trade was downing highballs. I spotted: Lady Jean and Annis listening to a stuffy dullard with chewed mustaches . . . Lord Everard surrounded by three females, eagerly hanging on his words . . . and David (with a drink) standing beside a merry-faced, gray-haired woman who was sipping tea and looking faintly restive.

I laid my course toward the Laird to bring me past the Campbells. "Lord Everard!"

He rose like a young trout to a fly. "Sable, lass, good to see ye," but from his kiss and happy twinkle, I knew he'd nothing to tell me yet.

On to Lady Jean for a hearty kiss, while chewed-mustaches rose politely. "Lord Camber," she said, with the vagueness of boredom. "Charles, here's Sable Gordon-Lennox. She's why ye're here." From her tone, I knew she considered him a sad mistake—and after shaking his limp hand, I felt she was right.

"Annis, darling, sorry to be late," I murmured, leaning to kiss her. "Tell you later."

Moving on to the Laird, I sensed David was not happy with me. His vis-à-vis perked up—hoping for rescue? "Sable," he said thinly, "we wondered if you'd forgotten us."

"By no means," I assured him, "but I was at Comynhaugh, and Sholto was wanted in the byre—" I smiled at Her Majesty's second cousin (it could only be she)—"so he bundled me off home with the dogs breathing down my neck."

She laughed heartily, extending a hand. "So you're the American cousin? Lord David, you're fortunate in your relatives."

"We think so, Lady Camber." The Laird was restored to smiles by her reaction. Throwing an arm about me, he announced, "Ladies and gentlemen, here's my young clanswoman from New York, Miss Sable Gordon-Lennox, whom you're asked to meet and welcome with us." David hugged me and kissed my temple. The guests stared at me. I knew that look:

151

hmmm, so this is the new one?

So David had a reputation? The "look" was limited to the businessmen, although Mrs. Lawson looked thoughtful. The other wives were evaluating my New York cocktail dress and thinking poorly of it, judging by their cordiality. I'd no idea how much David had drunk; it was enough to make me uncomfortable in the extreme, and I couldn't release myself. There was strength in that arm. I allowed myself to be conducted about and to be formally presented. He kept giving me gentle hugs and praising me for my speech, my photography, my general credit to the Clan—until Lady Camber and Lady Jean were looking *polite,* and I was ready to sink through the floor. . . .

Then Sholto, Earl of Aboyne and Sutherland, walked in and arrogantly plucked me from the Laird's grasp. "Give over, Davie, 'tis my turn now." Sholto cuddled me against him and laughed infectiously. "Och, we do naught but fight over who's to spoil her most—eh, Andrew?"

"That ye do, milord," the butler remarked severely, "the way she'll be totally above hersel' when she departs."

Amid the ripple of laughter, Sholto moved me away with him. "Now, where shall I tuck ye while I make my bows?" He pursed his lips. "Everard, ye're no' safe despite your age, but ye'll recall ye're my godfather?" I was deposited next the Lord Lieutenant, who instantly put his arm about me.

"In these matters, 'tis every man for himsel'," he stated austerely. "Come, lad—'tis the fairst thing I taught ye. Make your bows, and when ye return I may give her up, or I may not."

152

The awkward moment was receding in a wave of smiles and chuckles. Sholto sighed resignedly, "Och, weel, there's no good in the Campbells. 'Tis well known they're forever coming—but do they come, ye can never be rid o'them." There was a general burst of laughter, and he was off-bending over Annis's hand, leaning to kiss Lady Jean, asking gracefully of Lady Camber, "Ye'll permit me to drink tea with ye?"

I sat down shakily, accepting Andrew's cup of tea and small plate of sandwiches with a smile of confidence I was far from feeling . . . because right then I knew this was going to be a party to end all parties if something wasn't done. Sholto'd covered the first difficulty, but I could see the Laird jovially retreating with Lawson and Exeter.

"Excuse me a tiny moment?" I was on my feet, whipping after the trio, "David, may I have a word with you, please?" I smiled at the others: "Go along, I only want a minute. . . ."

David was furious, but I got in first, "*You* arranged this party, *you* invited Her Majesty's second cousin," I hissed viciously, "and *you* will make certain that no guest is unable to attend pre-dinner drinks in full command of his senses! Understand?"

I'd been right he could keep his head. He understood. "Have some coffee," I suggested. "You can lay the groundwork for whatever deal you're working on, but abandon the hard sell until midnight supper—by which time, they'll be twice as receptive for having successfully coped with all the formality."

"Midnight supper?"

"Welsh rarebit, coffee, beer, drinks—served when the ladies retire."

"Eh, ye're a clever luv," David fingered his chin slyly, while I backed away. "I'd forgot Lady Camber."

"Yes, I thought you had—what she sees is what Her Majesty may hear. Sober them up, sweetie!"

I went back to the kitchen. "Mrs. Frame, a pot of strong black coffee for the record room—three cups, no sugar or cream—and a plate of whatever's left of sandwiches. The Laird's aware his guests must do credit to Lady Camber," I added calmly, casting a glance about the kitchen. "Mrs. Frame, if you ever need a job, you're hired as of now," I said admiringly. "The organization, the way you've set everything for one-two-three! I never saw the like."

I left the kitchen. Presumably the Laird would now be capable of hosting his own dinner, but it was all taking far more energy than it was worth, I decided, going back to the tea tables. Lady Jean was chatting comfortably with Lady Camber. Sholto had got Lord Camber out to the garden, along with Mrs. Hampton-Smith and Mrs. Uppington. Lord Everard was chatting with Annis. The rest were setting aside glasses and cups, beginning to drift away to their rooms.

Lady Jean waggled an imperious finger. "Catherine, here's the grand-niece of the woman Cargill would have given his all to marry, could he have found a way to kill her husband," she chuckled.

"Not surprising, if looks run in the family," Lady Camber smiled. "So, you're photographing? What's pleased you best?"

"Lord Everard stomping along the howe," I said slowly. "A black lamb that didn't know which way he was going, so he stood bleating before my car until the ewe called him. Lady Jean's rock garden, and I *think*

154

I've a superb shot of Skiddaw. The clouds were just right."

"Nothing of London? I thought everyone photographed the Guards."

"I'm afraid I didn't, but," I said, "I was permitted to photograph Her Majesty with Prince Charles at Ascot, when I was presented by the Head of Scotland Yard. He's an old friend of my great-aunt."

Lady Camber's lips twitched slightly. "I shall hope to see some of your pictures. Not Ascot, I'm quite familiar with Her Majesty."

"Yes," I nodded, "so is everyone in the world actually—so I've only the one, I don't even know if it's any good."

She eyed me poker-faced for a minute. "I see what you mean," she remarked to Lady Jean and snorted happily, pulling herself to her feet. "My friends call me Lady Catherine, Sable." She smiled regally. "Jean, are you ready to dress for dinner?"

The servants were unobtrusively clearing away. Sholto had led the garden lovers to the center door, and dispersed them to their rooms. Annis had gone up with the titles. There was no sign of the Laird. "We served the coffee," Andrew said, "but they're still there."

I stalked down the hall, rapped sharply on the door and swung it open. "Sorry, David, but everyone's going to dress, and no matter what you're working on, it must wait until you've worked on dinner and the other guests. Come along. No arguments. . . ."

They came along. There were no arguments. They were sober.

As I reached the morning room, I realized I was bone weary. I sat on the edge of the folding cot, stripped off

155

shoes, stockings, jacket. . . .

I didn't wake till Nellie's urgent shake. "The Lady Annis has descended, your bath is waiting."

I'd never have made it but for Nellie.

She produced a small green pill. "Harmless, but it wakes ye up till ye're awake by yersel'." She whisked me into and out of a tepid bath and briskly got me into underclothing. I settled down to make up at Annis's mirror. By the time we were ready for The Dress, I was perking once more.

It was a masterpiece. I swirled to reproduce the magazine photograph, while Nellie stood aside. "Aye, 'tis like enough," she said critically. "I couldna quite get the back draping, the picture was no' clear, but 'twill do. Ye're satisfied?"

"Beyond words! Have you any idea of what this dress would cost, Nellie?"

"Aye," she said, taking the comb and brush from me and calmly arranging my hair. I sat fascinated by her skill. "It'd be twenty, maybe thirty, guineas."

Ninety bucks? No time to talk now. I dabbed perfume about, collected my evening pochette and said, "Come down, lurk in the hall for a minute, to see how it's received?"

We did not have to go so far. Stepping down the stairs, I met Sholto coming in from the courtyard. "Good evening, cousin," I smiled. "I trust ye approve my obedience? Green, ye said, did ye not? And clinging . . . ?" I reached the hall floor and waltzed down the hall.

For a moment he stood silently inspecting me, the deep blue eyes almost sad. Then he grinned broadly. "You're very lovely, cousin. Thanks to ye, Nellie!

156

Whatever she pays ye, I'll double it. Nay," he said softly, coming toward me, "I'll triple it for turning her into the despair of every other woman in the place!" Sholto laughed, setting his hands on my shoulders and turning me about once more.

I sensed Nellie had gone when I'd completed the turn. Sholto took an impetuous step forward; I was swaying toward him, wanting nothing so much as a kiss . . . when there was a raucous burst of laughter from the salon. Sholto straightened up, threw a light arm about me. "Come, cousin, you must make an entrance. . . ."

It was a nerve-wracking evening.

What am I saying? It was horrible!

The Laird took one glance at me on Lord Aboyne's arm and narrowed his eyes in fury. When I went over to sit by Lady Catherine and coo David into good humour again, Sholto glared at me from the other side of the room.

Annis was no help, although I wasn't surprised after another inspection of Lord Camber. It may be right that one should always team bores with bores at a party, but compared to Lord Camber, Annis was a Dorothy Parker.

Every business wife took a good look at Nellie's gown and loathed me.

Andrew was worried about the amount of liquor the business contingent was swilling, although David was sharply limiting himself.

I was discouraged by the amount of cocktail goodies they were gobbling. The hors d'oeuvres might prevent drunken guests, they could also stifle appetites—to say nothing of dulling any appreciation of my carefully planned menu.

Lord Everard was disturbed by telephoned news of some legal problem in his bailiwick.

And on top of everything else, Sholto altered the dinner seating.

When Andrew threw open the doors with the formal announcement, Sholto presented himself at my side, extending a courteous arm. "Cousin?"

"But you don't take me in."

"Here's the card," he said, holding it under my nose.

"Dammit, you've got the wrong one, somehow. You're supposed to take in Mrs. Uppington," I muttered violently, aware of Lady Catherine's tactful detachment beside me.

"Aye, but if I must have a harpy beside me, at least let me have one with something to say."

"I think that's one point for him, my dear," Lady Catherine murmured. "Though I've every confidence you'll even the score rapidly. Ah, Lord David, do we lead the way?"

The menu cards provided a tiny break in the general disaster. I'd taken pains to embellish personally, where possible: the Gordon coat of arms for David, a rock garden for Lady Jean, the British lion for Lady Catherine, and so on. The unknown had flowers, and there were flattering exclamations for my talent. But just as David was beaming affectionately, Lady Catherine picked up Sholto's card. I'd drawn a kilted man dancing with a green evening dress. No face, only the dress.

"How clever," Lady Catherine laughed, extending

158

the card to the Laird, who took one look and went sour again. "Isn't she?" he said evenly, but Lady Catherine was replacing the card before Sholto. She leaned forward to ask, "I must know why there's no face, Sable."

"'Tis obvious," Sholto said, surprised. "Who could do justice to it? Our cousin's too modest to try."

"That's point two for him, unless you speak up," she remarked.

"It's no point at all, but stymie," I returned disdainfully. "He's merely trying to avoid exposure. He would have me wear a green dress on the enticement of dancing a reel with him." I looked at her impressively. "He even threatened to buy it himself! It's only the dress he cares for, so why should I be in it?"

"Ye see my point? A harpy she is, but with plenty to say."

Lady Catherine chuckled. "Yes, honors even," she decided, turning back to the Laird, who was faintly soothed by my pertness.

Dinner moved along from smoked salmon to sherried consommé to baby shrimps in aspic. Turning formally from side to side for conversation, I found myself coping with Mr. Lawson during the entree. He was a pig-eyed, plump vulgarian, evidently a long-time crony of David's, and bent on discovering how far the Laird had gotten with me. I didn't like him at all, and but for Sholto's highhandedness, I wouldn't have been sitting here having to parry suggestive comments. The fact that a business woman may know all the gambits doesn't make them any more palatable. By the time he was chummily calling me Sable ("my friends call me Alf, Sable"), on the score that we were undoubtedly going to see a lot of each other, my anger was equally directed against Lord Aboyne who'd saddled me with this nasty man.

"I'm afraid it's hello and goodbye, Alf, although if I ever get back to England, I'll remind you we're friends. But I'm leaving Friday to visit the Campbells, and from there to Paris and Rome, then back to New York."

"Ah, that's what you think," he winked, "but Davie'll find a way to keep you. Sharp as a tack, he is! He'll think of something, never fear; he won't let *you* go that soon, ha ha! No, no, you don't know our Davie." Lawson drained his wine glass and looked about. Andrew was occupied with studying space. "Where the devil's the bottle?" Lawson said impatiently.

"It'll be along in good time," I told him. "Eat your squab—isn't it delicious? You have to say you like it, because I made up the menu." He was slightly disgruntled but continued his dinner. "D'you like the rice stuffing?" I asked. "Be honest, Alf, because I wasn't sure about it."

He sampled cautiously, took another forkful. "Very tasty," he approved. I prattled along artlessly about American versus English foods and firmly directed his attention to the fresh beans with water chestnuts. At long last his plate was clean; he'd enough food in him to absorb the alcohol. With a sigh, I ate what I could of my own dinner. "Entertain me please, Alf. What's your job?"

He told me. Men always do. If you can ask the right question, they'll talk for *hours*. Alf was still describing his duties as David's first-in-command: living in Liverpool, always on duty to carry out the Laird's orders. For the first time, Lawson was bearable. Then

160

plates and wine glasses were removed for the salad. "I must talk to Sholto now," I said. "We'll finish over dessert."

I'd have given much to eat my salad in silence, to consider what Alf had revealed. He'd said he'd known David for years, they'd been friends from the moment they met, and he'd always lived in Liverpool. Was Alfred Lawson out of the Laird's past, did he know who David Kirby-Gordon really was?

"Take the pucker off your forehead," Sholto said. "I didna set ye next me to be ignored."

"And I didn't set me next you at all," I returned spiritedly. "I was meant to be over there, cheering Marsh and Exeter."

He peered across the center flowers. "Aye, 'tis a dead spot," he agreed. "But why should I have been left a victim?"

"Because Mr. Uppington is important to David, and Mrs. Uppington would have been overcome to be seated beside an earl, to say nothing of the subtle flattery to Marsh and Exeter to flank the guest of honor."

Sholto nodded, finishing his salad. "Ye're very fond of David, aren't ye?" he observed, sitting back in his chair.

"I'm appreciative. He's been extremely kind to a stranger, although Agnes Ware's grand-niece is a parlay not to be missed," I murmured reflectively. "He's got the Lord Lieutenant, who'd not have come but for me. He's got Lord Camber, by dangling 'financial expansion'; and even if Aunt Agnes's advisers won't give him a penny, my presence proves legitimate possibility. A refusal will be simply an octogenarian whim. So I'm fond of David for giving me a splendid party, but I'll thank you to assume nothing. I've already had the curiosity—and the suggestions—from my right."

Sholto's face went murderous. "He dared. . . ."

"Why not? It was in your mind, cousin, either for fact or future, don't deny it," I said. "For your information, I do not pay my bills that way."

"Never!" he muttered violently. "Never did I think it, damn ye, damn ye. . . ."

I sensed that Lady Catherine had a well-bred ear cocked in our direction as Sholto spluttered wildly. This was all we needed, I thought; a row between the guest of honor and her kinsman, right under the nose of Her Majesty's second cousin! I was saved by Andrew, producing a parade of servants bearing dessert, followed by Steenie and the pipes.

I'd left music to Andrew, who'd evidently gone wild. There was something for everyone: first the Laird, then Lady Catherine, Lord Camber; "The Campbells Are Coming" for Lord Everard; followed by separate tunes for Lady Jean, Annis, and Lord Aboyne—all interspersed with the formal stepping about the table and ending with a special serenade to me. No denying the pipes are loud, and not everyone's choice. "Filthy racket!" Lawson said irritably, when they'd stepped about for the last time and disappeared with a final flourish. I could see the Laird and the English guests were equally relieved.

So was I. The pipes had taken up all the dessert-conversation time, and Annis was already looking about, catching the ladies' eyes to take us away.

I leaned shyly to Lawson. "Don't be too long, please?

We're stuck till you come out for coffee. Then the girls can go to bed, while the boys whoop it up over midnight supper."

"Yeah," the pig-eyes winked lasciviously, "but not *all* the girls, eh?"

"Perhaps not. Mrs. Exeter looks the jolly sort," I said, and went away while he roared with laughter. Standing aside for Lady Catherine's precedence, I faced Sholto; he was wearing his black murderous expression. For a second our eyes met, then he turned and sank into his chair again.

I sat beside Lady Jean, who asked, "What's wrong, child?"

"I'm not sure, but if Lord Everard gets a call from John Morrisy, he must tell me in private, nobody else!"

"The Yard? Lord, child, I dinna like this at a'."

"Nor I, but if it's a mare's nest, there's no harm done . . . and if it isn't, perhaps I'll ask a question. Even then, if the answer's right, I'll forget it."

"Ye'll be packed to leave at dawn Friday," she said firmly. "Better yet, Cargill will remove ye after the ball; Everard'll bring your car—I'll drive ours to Leckiehowe."

I could have kicked myself for so disturbing her. Why hadn't I remembered she was only younger than Aunt Agnes—which didn't make her young. "No, no, it's only a small thing. I may have accidentally stumbled onto a legal mess, that's all."

She looked at me keenly, but apparently I'd convinced her, for she settled back with a sigh and allowed me to light her cigarette. "Do your pretty, child; we'll have plenty of time to gossip in the next weeks."

The business wives were making the most of Lady Catherine, who was coping expertly by dispatching each one for *something* at the end of five minutes. She didn't even need to consult her watch. She was nearly through with them when I arrived. "Dear Mrs. Lawson," she was smiling regally, "we shall meet again soon, but please excuse me now, or I'll have no other chance to know Miss Lennox."

"Is royalty born knowing, or is there a course in gracious dismissal?" I ruminated, when we were alone. "And why isn't it generally available in universities, or is it meant to be an exclusive privilege reserved to the bluest blood—like swans?"

Lady Catherine chuckled, carefully setting her demitasse cup in the exact center of the other chair. "This would not guarantee privacy among American guests," she remarked. "Helpfulness is one of your most predominant national characteristics, and someone would be certain to helpfully remove that cup—but here, it will be respectfully left until a servant takes it away."

"If I know Andrew, it'll be the last one he clears. He may even forget it and have to return when it's realized there's a cup short."

She smiled. "Yes, obviously you've the staff tucked in your pocket, Sable—to say nothing of your cousin."

I flushed uncomfortably. "David goes overboard a bit, but," I looked at her directly, "it only because he hopes Aunt Agnes will lend money for expansion. I'm afraid that may be why Lord Camber," I couldn't control a tremble in my voice, "inflicted this . . . disaster on you, Lady Catherine. I'm so sorry."

"I see." Her lips curved slightly. "I don't know why

Camber came. *I* came to meet you. Jean Campbell and Rose Atherton said it'd be worth my while—and it is—but," she eyed me keenly, "I wasn't speaking of Lord David, Sable. I was referring to Sholto." My flush deepened to burning cheeks; I hung my head and feebly apologized for my nasty temper.

"No, no, my dear. Impertinence is one of the few pleasant privileges of royalty . . . and when a most eligible bachelor bribes the servants to rearrange a formal table to place a beautiful girl next him, and then has a public scene with her, we know what it means!" She laughed again. "My dear Sable, I don't know when I've been so entertained. It's particularly good to see Sholto waked up again. Keep it up, and you'll have the undying gratitude of all his friends! . . . Ah, Lord David, you've finally brought back the spice. We females were growing dull with each other."

"I can't believe anyone could ever be dull with Sable," the Laird protested gallantly, extending his arm.

I was up and around behind Lady Catherine's chair in a minute. "Take my place, David."

I snuck away to the powder room to wash my hands while the blush subsided. Lady Catherine was so wrong, I thought; apparently Sholto was only interested in being rid of me. I looked into the mirror, freshening my lipstick, and admitted to myself for the first time: I wished she was right. If that were the way Sholto meant to play it through this horrible party, it was at least a clever cover-up . . . better than David's unctuous affection. Let Lady Catherine believe she was seeing legitimate romance, rather than an infatuated married man. More than ever it was important for me to make the best possible impression, I thought suddenly, if that damned succession might end up in my own family.

All right, I'd play Sholto's game . . . and see how uneasy I could make him by my public response to his gambits!

I came back to the salon and found everyone regrouped to absorb the men. Lord Everard was still being bothered by his legal problem, shaking his head and expounding to Lord Camber and anyone nearby. I got another cup of coffee and drifted toward the group. "'Tis the devil and all," he was saying, "here's the only male illegitimate, naught but women born true—the title dies unless we can get it to the House of Lords for special recognition—and all because the man hadna time to marry before the boy is born, and never got another." He shook his head, exasperated. "Och, the legal expense!"

"But if he married the mother eventually, it legitimatizes the boy automatically," I said without thinking. "Doesn't it?"

There was one of those peculiar silences that occur at parties, in which my words were momentarily distinct before the other groups resumed their own conversations. I looked at Lord Everard uncertainly. "Or didn't he acknowledge parentage?"

"O'course, but it makes no difference wi' entail, Sable. Ye wouldn' know, 'tis different in the States," Lord Everard said instructively, "but here 'tis only the wedlock boy can inherit."

Lord Camber nodded solemnly. "It's only recently a man could legitimatize a bastard at all."

Their voices flowed on, but I heard nothing more—

because now I knew why it was vital to prevent my browsing in the files.

The Laird was not only an impostor. Even if he were David Kirby, he wasn't a legitimate heir. Somehow he had positive evidence that George Kirby was descended from the original bastard, whose issue could never, even right at this moment, assume an entailed title without an Act of Parliament. Then I remembered that one letter marked "discarded as illegible". . . .

That must have been the one that had clearly stated which of Carmela's boys had died.

I became aware of Annis saying pallidly, "Lady Camber, Lady Jean, nearly eleven—shall we retire so we may be fresh for the shoot? Mrs. Lawson, Mrs. Hampton-Smith, Sable . . . ?"

"Yes, I'm quite ready." I set aside my coffee cup, looked up to see David and Sholto standing shoulder to shoulder behind Lord Everard. Lord E. scrambled to his feet, saying, "Eleven, eh? I'm for bed, too; what about you, Charles? Clear eyes needed for the Glorious Twelfth!" He was bumbling away, while I stood frozen, immobilized by cold gray eyes, grim blue eyes—they knew I knew.

Chapter 11

The breakfast room was crowded with local people invited for the shoot. I faded into a corner with coffee and a muffin to plan the photography.

The aristocracy were in muted tweeds; the business wives were in smartly colored woolens: flamingo pink, stark white, vibrant purple. They might frighten the birds their husbands were too hungover to shoot, but they'd liven the film. I went up to Annis: "I'm going to work—outside shots of preliminaries, you know; see you later."

The timing was perfect: I was in place to catch the beaters bringing the dogs from kennels to courtyard. They waved jovially, the dogs strained at their leashes, and the whole group passed by like a scene from Tom Jones, except there were cars instead of horses. The servants were trotting out with picnic baskets, joking with the beaters, and at last the guests poured out the front door. Motion pictures finished, I was now ready for the color stills. "David—pose, please! Line up, and look Edwardian!"

He posed with docile, good-humor in striking attitudes while I moved rapidly for three angles. In none would the Laird's face be recognizable—he had managed the evasion with skill. "Thanks!" I went away to the dim side hall, unloaded and reloaded. I heard the cars moving away, and Sholto calling: "Sable? Where the devil is she now, Andrew? SABLE?"

"Yes, just a minute."

"Will you come on! Do you think of nothing but cameras?"

"What else is there to think of?" I handed the completed rolls to Andrew, turned on Sholto. "I've borrowed equipment and outstayed my welcome—as you've constantly reminded me—for a chance to film."

"I'll tell ye what else to think of," he snorted furiously. "That you are delaying the entire shoot! Nobody can begin until all are in place, and we've farthest to drive, because I was fool enough to place ye in the blind with the best view."

Silently I stowed equipment and got into the jeep. Racing bumpily along the upper field track, I saw tops of heads, tips of guns. Far off, the dogs gave tongue and were silenced. I'd not expected to share a blind with Sholto. We couldn't be angry for hours. "Sorry, I—didn't know," I said.

He nodded curtly. At the blind he transferred our gear, setting my shooting stick firmly in the ground. He gave a peculiar short piercing whistle and dropped down beside me. "D'ye know anything?"

"Yes—but not that."

And I did. Grouse blinds are trenches of hard-packed earth, disguised by shrubs and strung in a line opposite the coverts, which is the underbrush where the

170

birds breed. By August twelfth, they're deemed big enough to eat—but grouse and ptarmigan are very canny. If disturbed, they depart—not by addlepatedly taking to wing, but by scuttling through the brush or by flying low behind a bush screen.

In Scotland, the Glorious Twelfth is a ceremony. To be certain of sport, there are beaters flailing the underbrush until the birds are upset enough to rise, allowing each man in the first blind to take two shots. Then the birds are allowed to settle, the dogs retrieve. In about ten minutes the beaters start again, moving forward to set the flush for the second blind—and so on down the line. The only stupid thing about grouse is, once they're chivvied to the end of the covert, the survivors circle back to home nests, so the beaters can repeat the whole process.

It could take anywhere up to an hour between first and second shoots for any given blind, during which time one sips champagne, nibbles sandwiches and enjoys fresh air. As Aunt Agnes said, "What it *is,* is an aristocratic outing!"

Poised for the first flush, I blessed Sholto: because this was the only blind to curve for a clear view the length of the field I could even see the Laird and Lord Camber rising. . . .

The birds rose, the guns cracked once, twice, then were still as the dogs dashed forward and back. It took three cameras, but I'd got it! I readied for the second blind—that would be Lord Everard, though I couldn't see him; all the intervening blinds were in a straight line, the occupants hidden. Slowly, the shoot came toward us. I was huddled in the far corner, striving for angle shots as Sholto raised his gun. . . .

The first shoot was finished. "Breathing spell," he smiled lowering his gun. "Thirty minutes to let the birds settle." He lit our cigarettes and sat comfortably on the sod, stretching his long legs before him. "Does it meet your requirements, cousin?"

"I hope for a prize," I confided. "I'm not so used to movies, but whether or not, I'll have something to please Aunt Agnes, and a usable print for Mac-Danald."

"Is this *all* your life, cousin?" he asked curiously.

I sat silent, staring at his fingers curled about a cigarette. "I was to marry an Air Force captain. He was . . . killed, driving to the wedding."

Sholto put his hand over mine quietly. "Can ye no' love again?"

"I want to, but after Jeremy . . . I just don't know." I looked blindly across the field. "You're a bit like him," I said without thinking. "He liked dogs, and the country. . . ."

"You're a bit like Meg," he said after a moment. "Not looks. She was Irish—black hair, gray eyes, not so much formal education, but the same quick wits, the same—integrity." He took a final drag, crushed out the cigarette. "She was a WREN . . . trying to drag a kid to safety when the Jerries came back for a second strafe."

I turned my hand gently, and we sat palm to palm until the clear piercing whistle signalled the second shoot was beginning at the other end of the field. "How many are there?"

"Lunch after this, and one more."

I'd save the remaining film for afternoon light. Now I could observe the other blinds. If there were a bag prize, it might easily go to the Laird; the dogs were busy

172

after his shoot. But there was little to retrieve after the intervening shoots until it reached us. For a single gun, Sholto was a hot contender: six dogs trotted back, proudly!

"Good shot, cousin!" I praised heartily. "Lunchtime?" I looked up with a smile, only to have it fade into uncertainty at his expression. Sholto stood, gun in hand, his eyes sad—as they had been the night before when I'd come down in the green dress.

"Ye'll forgive me, cousin? I must speak to Geordie, I'll take ye along to David—or would ye prefer the Campbells?"

"The Campbells, please. . . ."

I leaned over Lord Everard and said dramatically, "I'm a desairted female, ye'll take pity on me and allow me to eat wi' ye? I brought my own vittles."

They helped me down, happily making space. Lady Jean said, "Och, ye'd fit anywhere, slim as ye are."

"Aye, I'll no' need compress mysel'," agreed Lord Atherton, a chubby little man with a twinkle in his eye, "and well inspect the contents of her basket, Everard. She may have summat we're missin'."

It should have been fun. It wasn't. Sholto'd given me the choice spot for a film, repaid my confidence with his own . . . but it was still a maneuver. Once accomplished, he'd no wish to eat lunch alone with me. After forty-five minutes, I couldn't take any more. "Forgive me? I'll wander back with what ye've left for poor Sholto—and catch a few pictures of the wildflowers upfield."

Trudging back along the cart tracks, I heard the sort of voices, titters, guffaws that said Uppington, Lawson, *et al,* were more occupied with the hair of the dog than the wing of the bird. I finished the roll in the still camera with landscapes, picked up the lunch basket, and dropped down into our blind, feeling tearful. There was no sign of Sholto. I readied the cameras for the final shoot. Standing in the curve of our blind, I checked my light meter. I could hear the odd piercing whistle; last chance . . . sooner than I'd expected.

I forgot problems braced against the rock at the curved end of our blind . . . getting the flush, hearing the guns crack, catching the plummeting birds, yet somehow aware of a *difference* in sound . . . as if two guns had fired once, one gun twice. . . .

The light meter slipped from my finger; I bent to pick it up . . . something whistled overhead, *pinged*. . . .

I fell forward and crawled into the corner, weeping uncontrollably. I heard a motor racing toward me. Sholto, coming back to see if he'd got me? I tried, but I couldn't compose myself before he was there jumping down—staring at me. "Sable, what is it?"

"Don't you know?" I sobbed wildly. "Someone shot at me—but Sholto, even if I knew anything, I wouldn't tell."

"What are ye talking about, lass? Shhh, it's all right, darling." He knelt beside me, pulled me against him, and wiped away my tears, murmuring gently, "Shhhh, there now. 'Tis only the guns, ye're not used to the sound."

I lay against him wearily, and we saw it together: a rifle slug that had hit the outcrop above the blind and now rested on the hard dirt floor.

Sholto's face went ghastly white. After a moment, he leaned forward to pick it up. "God damn all Sassenach commoners, who know naught of a gun," he said, deadly soft, and drew me against him once more. "'Tis meant to be the blank following the second shot, to prevent a man taking more than his bag in the excitement of the moment, d'ye understand?" I nodded weakly, and he stuck it in his pocket. "I'll have a word to say about this," he muttered. "If David canna choose guests who know the rules, he'll provide loaders for each blind henceforth."

I was incapable of speech. Did he really think it had been one of the English guests? It was the Laird himself. I even knew how he'd done it: he had shot with Lord Camber. That was the difference I'd sensed in the sound. He'd seen me filming from the curve of the final blind; he'd stood to the rear of the first blind, taken one shot, and when all eyes were breathlessly looking forward, he'd swivelled and timed the slug to coincide with Lord Camber's second shot. . . . If I hadn't bent down for the light meter, he'd have got me straight through the forehead.

I wondered who would have been blamed? Whoever the Laird liked least; and who, once the incident was discreetly hushed would be forever indebted to David. Clever!

"What don't you know that you wouldn't tell if you did?" Sholto asked softly.

"It's only an old diary, about a shoot for Edward VII, but I don't know who Lady P was, Sholto. Isn't it time for you?"

"Mphmmm." He withdrew his arm and stood up. The dogs were only now returning (dispiritedly) from the flush for the previous blind. Sholto picked up his gun, examined it, sighted, made ready. I looked at my toes, fumbled for a cigarette—and found Sholto waiting to light it. I looked at the heather below us, at the gorse on the hillside, at my toes again—but of course it was no use.

"What, no more pictures, cousin?" he asked, hurt. "I'm not worth a finale? Come now, it'll be my best, I promise ye."

"I've no more film. Attitudinize, and let me enjoy the spectacle."

For a second his blue eyes flashed at me while the birds were flushing. Then he turned and took his two shots almost at random. He lowered the gun, not even glancing at the tumbling specks caught in the sunlight. "Now you'll tell me why David should try to kill you," he said softly.

I scrambled to my feet, collecting cameras. "Oh, nonsense! Nobody tried to kill me, sweetie. It was only an accident. I was a bit shook up, but no harm done, after all."

His hand caught my wrist, and if I had thought David strong, this man was iron. "Look at me." I looked. "He's a womanizer in his cups," Sholto said. "Did he . . . attack you, Sable?"

"No! Oh, I know he drinks, maybe he'd rather I didn't report it," I said. "But there's many a man only functions with alcohol after a deal is done."

In the distance I could hear cars coming forward, stopping at each blind, picking up occupants, moving away. "Very well, play the hand your own way." Sholto dropped my wrist. "But watch yourself, cousin. Shall we go?"

I couldn't face tea. "Tell the Laird I'm dispatching the film." When Mrs. Frame's back was turned, I filched a jar of jam.

And then to Strathbogie. "If I present this to Bess, would she give me a cup of tea?"

You don't fool a Bess MacDanald. After Ranald left to go to the shop, she asked, "What are ye needing, the way ye come here for tea when there's a party at Strathmuir?"

"A private phone."

"John's away, gone north no more than an hour since," Eileen Morrisy said over the phone. "Is it important, Sable? His secretary'll reach him, if need be."

"No, it was only . . . I wrote, asking for information, but probably he hadn't time."

"Information? Oh, never fear, he'll have set someone to it," she said. "Ye'll know by morning probably."

But if the Laird had tried to kill me that very day, would morning be soon enough?

What was he going to do when I turned up unharmed? Sholto had the slug. Would he have spoken to David about it?

It *could* have been Sholto who'd taken a potshot . . . then dashed back to soothe me when he realized I wasn't dead. . . . He'd had an immediate explanation: inexpert guests . . . or a conjectured rape for which the Laird might wish to shut my mouth forever.

I crawled into the Austin-Healey and thought, "Why don't I just *leave?* I've some cash, my passport, traveler's checks. . . ." I sat for the duration of a cigarette in the driver's seat, then headed back to Strathmuir. A Gordon never retreats, never compromises, even at risk of his life—and even after that slug that afternoon, I couldn't entirely believe. . . .

You had better believe! my mind said grimly. Sholto put you into that one blind, nicely set up for David . . . if you hadn't left the Campbells on your own, he'd have brought you back—and found another reason to leave you alone. Think it through: you weren't meant to be found until time for Sholto's final shoot. David (or Sholto himself) was supposed to time that single shot to be unheard in the shoot from an intervening blind. Either man was a dead shot, I knew that now. And seeing me standing alone, for once David had taken the gamble of trying for me on his own shoot.

And because it wasn't supposed to be then, Sholto had loused up any second try by coming back too soon. Cynically I admired his quick explanations and removal of the evidence; and I bet he *had* said a word to David for jumping the gun! The shoot was the best chance they had; it was gone . . . and by tomorrow morning I'd be gone. If only my letter had reached Morrisy in time!

I left the car in the garage court, went up the rear stairs and gained my room without meeting anyone. I could hear indistinct voices, sounds of dressing for dinner, and there was a thin line of light under the Laird's door at the end of my hall. I doused my lights, locked the door and sat smoking in darkness. I heard Annis being dispatched from her room across the way . . . Nellie retreating to prepare for me.

Now, in the stillness, I remembered Sholto's anguished, "Shhh, *darling* . . ." and his white face when he saw the slug. Was that because he knew I'd seen it, too—or should it have been a blank, intended only to

178

frighten? Had my tale of "Lady P" been convincing? And—if Sholto reported it to the Laird—would David accept it?

There was a soft rat-a-tat on the morning room door. "Sable?" David's voice. I sat silent, praying Nellie wouldn't emerge till he'd gone.

She didn't.

She arrived a split second after his footsteps had died away. I knew by her averted eyes she'd heard his knock. Silently she extended another green pill, got me bathed and dressed and expertly did my hair in a completely different fashion. "For a reel, it must be more secure, the way ye'll not lose too many pins." When at last I was finished, she said, "Ye'll wait for me to undress ye, mistress, the way we'll know ye're secure."

"Thank you, Nellie."

But there was more than rape on David's mind if he realized I suspected imposture. I set my teeth and went slowly toward the stairs. I'd be safe enough among the guests; Nellie'd see me locked in for the night—but it was a flimsy ornate lock, easily forced or silently turned by no more than eyebrow tweezers.

So I wouldn't stay in the room. I'd dress again when Nellie had gone and sneak out—where? The garage and my car, I decided. It'd take a bit of time for David to look about the house; if he thought to search outside, I could make a dash for it.

I shivered uncontrollably, but at least I had a plan. I went down and caught Andrew in the rear hall. "Kinsman, ye'll not ask me why, but ye'll see my car is left unobstructed at evening's end?"

"We've another cot; Nellie shall sleep wi' ye," he returned baldly.

I couldn't risk Nellie's life. . . . "No, no, 'tis not so serious, Andrew—merely that I'll like perhaps a wee trip early in the morning."

"Aye. Sandy'll be at hand; give him a shout do ye need anything." Andrew went away, but I knew he still thought I was fearing rape . . . which was an interesting sidelight on the Laird's reputation among his own staff! I turned toward the solarium, and heard steps behind me in the record room hall: David? I whirled, half-choked with fright. But it was Sholto and Lord Everard, in close conversation, their faces grim with shock. The Lord Lieutenant's arm lay affectionately about his godson's shoulders; Sholto's head was bent respectfully. I looked at the two men, and I simply *knew* Lord Aboyne was unaware, was playing *no* game in partnership with the Laird. He'd not have Lord Everard's trust or confidence otherwise. The Lord Lieutenant was no man to be fooled!

I stood still, pressed against the wall. *Can ye no' love again, cousin?* Yes, that I could—and there he was . . . remembering lovely Irish Meg who gave her life trying to save one. Why hadn't I asked Sholto the same question? Could he possible love again? Could it be me?

They looked up, saw me, and stopped momentarily. "Why the long faces?" I asked gaily. "A poor start for a party!"

Lord Everard came forward shaking his head ruefully. "Ye're right, lass! 'Tis only I've the word o'complications in that case—but 'twill wait for tomorrow."

Sholto was already extending his arm with a smile.

"Always more beautiful, cousin! How d'ye contrive this?"

"'Tis the nature o'females," Lord Everard piped. He shouldered Lord Aboyne aside. "Gie over, lad, I'll have the honor tonight."

"'Tis I will have the honor," I announced. "I'll take the both of ye, this way we'll emphasize my importance!" I slid my arms into theirs, and we paced forward very grandly, suiting our steps to Lord Everard's. It was most definitely An Entrance, masterminded by Lord Everard, who stopped in the doorway, drew himself erect and looked about arrogantly.

"Campbell has come," he announced, "supported by Gordon and Aboyne. Ye may now admire us—and when ye're finished, we'll accept a wee drappie."

There was a ripple of laughter. The Laird was moving toward me, but well in front of him was a large beaming man, striding forward, arms outstretched. "Och, ye're the image! Go away, lads—now I'll have that kiss I never got!" I could see a mistiness in the Duke of Cargill's eyes, despite the bluff words. I abandoned Sholto and Lord Everard to kiss him heartily.

"I'm a poor substitute!" I said.

"Nay, nay, ye restore ma youth, lassie! Go away, David! Introductions? The fewer she knows the better; I'm keeping her for mysel'," the Duke boomed, hustling me across the room. "Beth, now ye'll see yer competition, and I trust ye'll be properly impressed."

The Duchess was white-haired, blue-eyed and beautifully fine-boned. We looked at each other critically. "I think ye had the best of the bargain," I told the Duke. "Had ye had my Aunt Agnes, there'd have been some famous fights, no doubt—but 'tis no' comfortable for a marriage."

Lady Cargill's lips twitched. "Ye've heard o' my husband?"

"No. My Aunt Agnes is not one to reveal the secrets of her heart—but by the look of him, he's irascible."

"For that, ye'll lean over so *I* can kiss ye," she decided, while her husband guffawed delightedly. "Didn't I tell ye? The quick tongue, the wit! Och, 'tis Agnes over again! Come, lass, sit ye doon. . . ."

I felt a strong arm about me. "Ye had your chance thirty-five years ago," Sholto said, eyeing the Duke coldly. "'Tis my turn now. Come awa', cousin, afore Alex lures ye into the garden. One thing ye must know about a Scot, lass," he instructed me, "he's *never* too old!"

"Oh, good!" I said briskly, cutting across the laughter. "Then perhaps you'll take me into the garden?"

His fingers tightened briefly, then relaxed. "Perhaps," he said cautiously, "if ye reel to my satisfaction —but I'm no' keen oh a forward lassie. I'll choose ma own time, ye ken?" He turned to the Laird. "David, ye'll take her other arm, the way we'll control her. I'd no idea the Colonies produced such wild ones."

"David!" I whirled, smiling, "where've you been?"

"Waiting my turn for a kiss," he laughed along with the group about us. But his eyes were cold as seashore pebbles. "If you're handing them out, I'll concede precedence to a Duke—but I still come before a lowly Earl."

"Don't tell me there's a protocol for kissing over

here?" I said, amazed. "Where I come from, we say 'pucker up'—and the hell with dukes and earls!" I put my arms about him lightly. "You're my Laird; you'll always come first." I managed it. I'd caught him a bit off guard. I was able to kiss his cheek warmly, hug him, and stand back smiling. His eyes flickered. He was wondering. . . .

Sholto's fingers gripped my elbow, and I reassured him: "You'll get yours in the garden, I'm not so furnished with kisses I'll waste any. Except one—for my Lady." I went across to Annis, who was sitting beside Lady Catherine. I smiled, leaning to kiss her. "How lovely you look, Annis darling! Lady Catherine, may I sit with you?"

She nodded regally toward the next chair, and I sat down. "Ah, Sholto! I thought you might be at hand," she said, extending her glass. "I believe I shall have a second drink after all."

It was going to be a good party: The English contingent, outnumbered by kilts and titles, were putting their best foot forward. I was beginning to relax. I no longer thought there was a sinister cabal between Sholto and the Laird. My happy greeting had made David uncertain; which argued that Sholto had said nothing of the shot. David couldn't be sure I had even been aware of it. If I could follow up. . . . I had a sudden idea. . . .

"Oh, Sholto—a drink? Do I *dare?*"

"Yes," he said calmly, sitting cross-legged on the floor before Lady Catherine and myself. "I mean to ply ye with liquor till I'm sure of that kiss."

"I thought she'd none to spare?" she observed.

"Oh, come now, Cathy," he protested. "One look

183

and ye know this one's made of kisses. There must be a few crumbs about the edges for a hungry man."

"Hungry for what? There's enough provender for a Bothwell rebellion on those tables!"

"Cathy, how can you be so *crass?* Sure, your values have changed since ye married that Sassenach! Ye forget the food for the spirit . . . forbye, there's a full moon tonight, and ye know how that affects the Sutherlands!"

"Oh, no, you mustn't bay, Sholto—it'd upset Jennie. She's only just whelped," I explained earnestly to Lady Catherine, who laughed.

"I don't know who's ahead, you're moving so fast I've lost count for the fun of watching," she complained.

"If you were versed in American comedy routine, you'd know that Who is always on First," I told her, setting aside my glass and rising. "You'll excuse me? Time for the pretty. . . ."

I caught the Laird's arm. "There are people I haven't met, people to rearrange . . . Mrs. Lawson, Mrs. Uppington dying of boredom . . . come along, sweetie." We broke apart the friendly cliques as well as the dead pockets, raised the noise level ten decibels, got the buffet line started, and ended near the garden windows.

David surveyed his party: people were happy, animated, mobile. "Eh, you're a clever girl," he grinned at me. "Come out for a breath of air?" He'd swung open one of the glass panels. . . . All at once Sholto was beside us. "Come away at once! Ye'll no' sit under an apple tree with anyone else but me, cousin."

"There's no apple tree in the garden," David frowned.

"Och, weel—we'll find summat."

"Fairies at the bottom of the garden," I said, "or *is* there a bottom? It seemed quite level, now I think of it."

"Which is more than can be said of you, cousin: all curves, the better to fit a man's arm, eh, David?" Sholto laughed, pulling me against him. "Come away, and I'll feed ye."

"I'll need sustenance to cope with you!" I agreed. "Come along, David—protect me from this madman."

By dinner's end, I'd nearly forgotten the Laird in self-defense. Wherever I sat, whenever I moved, Sholto was at my elbow. He was perfectly outrageous, and all the Scots were egging him on. With my damnable fair skin, he had me blushing furiously, until the only way out was to throw caution to the winds. At least I stopped blushing in the concentration of giving as good as I got.

The music began—it was a Viennese waltz. I may be tone-deaf, but I feel rhythm, and once I've looked at the footwork, I can do anything from a tango to a Watusi. The Duke of Cargill was pulling rank. "Lord David, ye'll open with Lady Camber—and I should dance with Annis, but," he held out his hand to me, "ye'll forgive my nostalgia. Sholto, deputize for me? Come, lass."

The Laird glided away with Lady Catherine for a circuit of the ballroom, while the Duke waited impatiently for the halfway mark, his arm already around me, ready to go.

Go we did, with couple after couple following, until the floor was filled. And if anyone got in the Duke's path, he moved 'em down. Wow, could he waltz! When the music stopped, he smiled. "Ye're near as good as

185

she," he conceded graciously. "Eh, I made a rare fool o'myself that night, but ye'll tell Agnes I never regretted it. 'Tis not every man can have a superb wife—and a lovely memory."

"I'll tell her," I promised. "And I'll tell you, she has never forgot, either . . . because she has never told—not even me!"

When the music began again, David's voice said, "Sable?" and Sholto protested, "No, I'm next!"

"This is no reel," I said severely, going into the Laird's arms. "Come back when it starts, laddie. David darling, let's go!"

"Are you enjoying yourself, my dear?"

"Immensely!"

"Did you get your film of the shoot?"

"Yes, and it'll be superb! Oh, it was heavenly, every minute!" I prattled on. "Who got the best bag?"

"Lord Camber. I believe I was runner-up," the cold gray eyes twinkled frostily. "Sholto usually outshoots me, but it seems his mind wasn't entirely on it today . . . nor tonight, for that matter."

"Oh, he's only a bit flown; I don't mind—it's rather fun," I said comfortably. "How about you, are you pleased with the way it's going?"

"Yes. You did an excellent job," he remarked. "What shall we do when you're gone, I wonder?"

"Regina MacLaren," I said. "Monday and Thursday at ten, shorthand rusty, typing excellent, glad of money to put by for the boy's medical school." I chuckled at David's blank face. "She was private secretary to the Duchess of Norfolk before marriage. The Women's Institute thought she'd be exactly right for Annis."

"I see." He smiled faintly. "You've made—quite a

change in our lives, Sable."

Now. . . .

"For the better, I hope. David, this may be our last private moment," I said soberly. "I've things to say, some pleasant—perhaps some impertinent."

"Nothing could be impertinent between us, Sable."

"First, my sincere thanks for all you've done, David . . . and second, after meeting your business associates, I know you have what it takes of executive ability to make a success of any project. So I shall break the rule and tell Aunt Agnes to help."

"Thank you, my dear—but what's impertinent about that?"

"Third," I said steadily, "I never knew the legal ramifications of entail until Lord Everard explained last night—but if you've been worrying about 'Lady P'—don't!"

Not what he'd expected! "What are you talking about, Sable?"

"That diary . . . and you didn't want me ferreting in the record room," I said. "I couldn't think *why* until last night." I looked at him squarely. "You've been thinking Lady P was Penelope Gordon, the old Laird's mother, and worrying that perhaps he was illegitimate, haven't you?"

David eyed me impassively; I didn't blink. "Go on," he said.

I shrugged. "Waste of time to worry. Even if the title should have gone elsewhere sixty years ago, it's back where it belongs, isn't it?"

He drew a sudden deep breath. "Yes—although how you twigged it so quickly!" He shook his head in admiration. "I've been uneasy for years, Sable . . .

187

didn't dare consult anyone for fear of a legal mess, but you really think it doesn't matter?"

"Not in the least. Whoever should have been here then, you'd still be here now," I pointed out reasonably. "Everybody in between is dead. I think I won't even tell Aunt Agnes, David. It's far too nebulous, no proof at all—just a fun-suspicion for the two of us?" I grinned at him wickedly, and slowly his lips curved in that sly smile.

"Sable, Sable!" he sighed deeply, hugging me close for a moment. "You'll never know the relief!" He laughed softly. "I should have had you years ago."

"Not really. Annis was what you needed, you need her still," I said absently, watching Sholto prancing about with Mrs. Exeter who obviously adored him. "Once she has Regina MacLaren, she'll do nicely, you'll see." I looked at David's blank expression. "Annis *loves* you, didn't you know?" I asked curiously. I knew by the flicker of his eyes he didn't. I'd a sudden hunch: Go for broke!

"She's easily confused by your quicker mind, afraid of your impatience when she can't keep up," I said. "Big successful men sometimes outgrow the pretty girls they married . . . but something tells me you're tied to Annis by more than a legal bond, David. I suspect you love her." I smiled at him affectionately. "Could you try telling her so, once in a while?"

The music ended. The Laird held me in his arms, looking half-uncertain, half-hopeful. "If only you're right," he muttered.

"Oh, I am, never doubt it, sweetie!"

Lord Everard was tapping David's arm imperiously. "The music's ended, and I'm engaging Sable for the next dance. Forbye, I canna trip wi' ma lame knee, so we'll sit it out," he announced. "Y'see, there's grand compensations to growing old, David. Come, lass."

The Laird dropped his arms slowly. "Thank you, Sable—for everything. . . ."

I sat between Lord Everard and Lady Cargill, chatting sociably and fuming inwardly because I wanted to talk to the Lord Lieutenant alone . . . although obviously he knew nothing. I could only hope I'd confused the Laird sufficiently to get away tomorrow in safety. He didn't know the Family Tree, he might accept the red herring. He wouldn't be able to check in the record room until the party ended . . . and might not remember which diary I had used. Even then it would take him a while to discover that the old Laird was at least a year old at the time. . . .

The band was going away for the break, the pipers were marching in, and Sholto was bowing gracefully over Lady Catherine's hand. "Ye'll excuse me, Cathy? 'Tis the moment I've awaited. . . ."

"So have we all," she remarked. "Heaven knows, there's been enough talk about it."

The pipes were warming up, the sets were forming, and Lord Aboyne stood before me. "Cousin, will ye reel with me?"

"Anytime!"

It had been years since I'd done a Scottish reel, but it came back to me with Sholto's strong hand to set me right once or twice. Lord Camber partnered his wife expertly, while Annis twirled with the Duke, and David bobbled around stiffly but adequately with

189

Lady Atherton. But it was Sholto who was the focus, whose grace made every man do his best, whose blue gaze was wickedly tempting. . . .

We reeled. We flung. Then we sat breathless while the men brought punch. Annis was sweetly flushed, talking to someone, with David's arm about her protectively. His eye caught mine briefly, in a genuine smile, and I thought perhaps it'd be all right after all. . . . The pipes warmed up again, and Andrew produced swords for Sholto.

"Ye'll no' let him display wi' no competition?"

"Dance with him, if ye can," he said, setting the swords neatly.

"You think I can't?" I demanded hotly.

"Nay, I think ye can," Andrew murmured. "Go to it, lass!"

Sholto was already stepping from quarter to quarter, the Duke and Lord Everard loudly acclaiming his agility. I looked at the Earl of Aboyne and Sutherland. . . . A bit drunk he might have been, but beautiful he was, and did he want to display for the company; so I'd display for him. In a split second I'd gathered my skirts into one hand and faced him. "Ye'll no dance alone, cousin—anything's better do ye have a woman with ye. . . ."

It's easier with kilts, but somehow I managed it, skipping back and forth until the pipes died and Sholto leaped forward, catching me in his arms, swinging me high and laughing heartily. "Och, ye canna do anything without a Gordon must demonstrate, too!" He set me back to the floor in the midst of laughter and clapping. He threw his strong arm about me, stepped over the swords and turned to the others: "Charles, Cathy, ye'll

190

never let me walk away unchallenged? Atherton, where are ye? Andrew, more swords! Cargill, are ye grown old, the way ye're sitting still? Everard, ye're judge!"

The pipes began again; the Duke was on his feet, spluttering, while Lord Atherton pulled his wife forward.

Sholto led me through the long windows to the garden . . . silently, quietly, along the paths. . . . "Here's the bottom o' the garden, but I'm afraid there's no fairies, nixies, leprechauns—only myself."

"What's wrong with that?"

You never know you're a woman till you've a man's arms around you. The instant Sholto's lips met mine, I went wild. I was clinging to him, stroking his hair, holding him against me, everything forgotten in the joy of the moment.

"Sable, you sweet child," he murmured.

"I'm not a child."

"I'm old enough to be your father, for all ye're a tempting reminder of youth," he said lightly.

"Oh, come now—you said a Scot was never too old, but fifteen's a bit young for paternity," I scoffed, pulling him close. After a moment: "You see a kiss is always a kiss, it has nothing to do with age."

"Ye're daft," he said harshly, pushing me away. "Go home, cousin. Find yourself a young man to cope with your humors." He moved away to lean against a topiary tree, his face averted.

"Must I, Sholto?"

"Aye, ye must."

"All right, I'll try—but it's a bit *much* to be a two-time loser," I said tremulously. "So I've red hair and green eyes . . . you don't look like Jere, either, but if I can forget him, why can't you forget Meg?"

Sholto swung around. "You don't understand. . . ."

"No, I don't understand wasting a life for a shadow, but if that's your choice, may it make you happy."

The orchestra was back, the floor crowded, and I took the first free male arm, which turned out to be that of Hampton-Smith. "Dance with me?" Over his shoulder, I saw Sholto coming back through the garden doors.

Sholto moved to the edge of the dancing and stood still until Hampton-Smith brought me alongside. He stepped forward and said, pleasantly, "Thanks, old chap—I'll take back ma girl, now,"—and there I was, buried against Sholto's shoulder.

"Pull together, lass," he said, softly authoritative. "We've still to finish this damnable evening, with half the commoners already wobbling."

I pulled together, and at a glance I saw he was right. Hampton-smith was the best of the lot, but catching up fast; Exeter was stoned, Lawson was laughing too loudly, and the Laird was squeezing Mrs. Uppington and murmuring something suggestive, judging by her giggle.

"'Twill end in a shambles, so ye'll dance with Cargill, Camber, Atherton or myself," Sholto stated. "Ye'll sit beside Everard if ye lack a partner, and ye'll not dance again with David, even if ye must pretend ye've wrenched an ankle and cannot dance with anyone. Ye understand?"

"Yes."

The music ended. "Ye'll forgive the moon-madness, cousin? I was a bit . . . flown," he said quietly, "but it's I who's the two-time loser, darling. You'll find a young man,"—he dropped his arms, smiling faintly—"for I'm too old to hope for your like again. Everard. I've brought her back to ye, which is a privilege far beyond your desserts. You'll excuse me, cousin?"

I sat silent, as he went away to speak with Andrew and disappeared into the hall. Lady Catherine's voice said plaintively, "Well?"

"He says he's too old, did you ever hear anything so silly?"

"Men are silly. I expect you'll have to tell him, Sable."

"Oh, I shall, never fear!"

"Let me be the first to welcome you, cousin." She smiled mischievously. "I'm a Sutherland, too."

"Oh, good! The thing is," I frowned, "if I have to compromise him, would you have to object?"

She laughed. "Just say when, where and how; every Clan will assist! Yon bachelor'll be trussed and delivered to ye at the altar, if need be. Ye'll be happy as grigs—which is more than I'll say for this affair. Charles, I believe it's time to withdraw." She stood up. "Perhaps you'll like a nightcap?"

"Perhaps, but first I'd like one dance with Miss Lennox."

"Of course." We moved away, leaving a general departure behind us. I suddenly realized Lady Catherine *had* to retire; nobody could leave before Royalty!

The Laird and Annis were shaking hands of departing guests, motors were coming forward in a line to the courtyard steps.

193

Lord Camber was making stuffy conversation: first trip to Scotland? Going on to France, eh? Must stop to see us on your way, near King's Lynn. . . .

"Thank you, I'm staying with the Campbells for a bit. I want to make the most of Scotland while I'm here."

"Of course, but you'll soon be back." I looked up, startled to encounter a broad wink. "I shall have one nightcap," he smiled, "and retire for the next installment in Project Sholto."

I giggled helplessly; how had I ever underestimated this man! He was bringing me around toward the hall door—and the music was suddenly a waltz. The Duke of Cargill beamed at us. "I'll replace ye, Charles, for a final whirl."

We had the floor almost to ourselves, with everyone wisely scooting out of the Duke's way. "That's enough for an old man," he said finally, coming to a stop near the door. "Thank ye for humoring ma sentimentality, lass . . . but 'tis only good night, not goodbye. Everard and Jean'll bring ye to Leckiehowe one day before ye leave." He kissed me heartily. "Go along wi' ye, sleep well!"

I started along. "But you're not going, Sable? I want another dance," David muttered.

"Can't, sweetie," I muttered in return. "Camber stepped on my toes. It was all I could do to manage that waltz with the Duke."

Lord Everard was beside me. "What's amiss, Sable?"

"We'll limp upstairs together, that's what," I said. "If I don't get out of these shoes and massage my feet, I'll have to be carried out of here tomorrow morning! David," I smiled at him mistily, "thank you from the bottom of my heart!" I kissed him gently. "See you tomorrow, darling . . . and stop worrying!"

Leaning on Lord Everard's arm, I looked back from the top of the stairs—and met David's watchful eyes. Had I convinced him that I knew nothing? I gave him a final smile, blew him a kiss and limped away to Annis's morning room.

Chapter 12

Where was Sholto? There was no sign of him among the departing guests in the lower hall.

Readied for bed by Nellie and locked into the morning room, I felt a bit desperate. I was to leave the following morning at ten; I felt certain Sholto had made tracks to hide at Comynhaugh until I'd gone, but how could I leave until I'd got it straight? He would take good care we'd never meet again. He'd go to Skye, the Orkneys, the Outer Hebrides, *someplace*.

Was he letting me down easily, pretending it was only the difference in age? In the darkened room I sat spelling my thoughts with a cigarette. Below, there was a final burst of music, raucous laughter, jovial shouts. The party was over. The ballroom lights flicked out one by one, leaving darkness on lawns and shrubs.

Lady Catherine thought Sholto loved me; she thought it a good idea, even if I had to make him marry me. I went over the moments in the garden, and I couldn't be mistaken. I was no silly teen-ager, I *knew* what love felt like . . . and I knew that man loved me. I crushed out the cigarette, turned on a light; my mind was made up. I decided to find Andrew, get directions for Comynhaugh and go after Sholto right then!

There was a knock at the door. "Sable?" Annis's voice. I opened the door to find her holding a small tray with one cup. She looked faint with weariness. "Your chocolate. Traditional on Opening Day . . . David was annoyed with me for forgetting, but since your light was on," she sighed, "well—here it is."

"How kind of you." I set the tray on a table, took a tiny sip politely, and gently urged her back to her own room. "Go drink your own chocolate, darling. Cheer up, it's nearly over!" I stood smiling, until she'd closed her door. There was light beneath the door at the end of the hall: the Laird was in his rooms. I was no longer worried about him. Let Morrisy handle it when he had time. I whipped into my clothes, not stopping for makeup. As I collected gloves, scarf, handbag, I saw the cup of hot chocolate. There was already a skin forming as it cooled. Oh dear, and Annis had gone to the trouble of bringing it—I suspected she'd made it herself to please David, but it was horridly bitter. I opened the window and quietly emptied the stuff onto the ivy, catching my breath at the moonlit beauty of the fortalice. Irresistible! I grabbed a camera, found the night film, turned off the lights and was out and away.

Quick as I thought I'd been, the staff had been even quicker. All was dark and silent when I felt my way to the kitchen. I couldn't blame them; my watch said five to three. All the same it was a major frustration. I'd no idea where Andrew slept and couldn't wake everyone by creeping about. Was anyone still up? I slid out the rear door, hopefully, but the servants' wing was dark, and even as I looked, the final light of Strathmuir went out—in the Laird's room.

Damn the man and his "tradition"—but for his forcing poor Annis to make me that cup of chocolate, I'd have been five minutes earlier. I would surely have caught someone still awake. Now what? Sandy, in the garage! I trotted up the garden steps to the court, where my car sat unobstructed as promised, but judging by the magnificent basso profundo snores rolling forth from his room, it would take more than a wee shout to rouse Sandy. Maps somewhere? I poked about; there were no maps. Of course not. Everyone but me knew how to get to Comynhaugh, and if I hadn't been so thrilled to be driving with Sholto, I'd have watched the turns more carefully that day. Then I'd be able to get there, too.

Could I possibly remember if I tried? I sat in the passenger seat and concentrated. We'd gone the other way from Strathbogie. I thought we'd generally gone left at crossroads and I knew we hadn't crossed the river. Not good enough, and there was no point in getting lost at three-thirty in the morning. I choked down disappointment and tried to think positively: Wait for dawn, Georgie Milkman . . . or Sandy might be awake . . . probably *better* for me to arrive at breakfast instead of showing up, wild-eyed with determination, in the middle of the night. Men are nearly always more tractable when fed, and I had a hunch it would take ingenuity to catch this particular lad.

The night air was crisp, exciting, matching my own excitement. It was hard to wait, because so far as I was concerned I was going to marry Sholto Comyn whether or not he wanted a wife! I'd sit in the car until first light, then drive down to intercept the milkman. . . . I tried just sitting—for a whole cigarette, but I was too excited to stand it. The moonlight on the fortalice was luring me. I got out of the car, slung the camera around my neck and made my way leisurely up the hill from the garden. It was not so much for the photographs as a febrile need to move, to contemplate the joy of loving once more.

Above me the fortalice was rugged, protective, somehow it symbolized Sholto himself. I remembered the day he'd carried me down, the feel and smell of him, and I shivered all over with anticipation. I took a few pictures here and there, until finally I was on the plateau, running my hand absently over the weathered stones, lost in a dream world.

I was already choosing names for our children.

The boys would be Hamish and Sandy; the girls, Chloe and Agnes. If there were more than four (at the moment I was uninhibited), Sholto could decide their names.

One can be drunk with more than alcohol. . . .

I went into the fortalice and looked up to watch the moon descending into the oblivion of day. Strangely, the spiral stairs were no longer frightening in this soft light. Without thinking, I went up, fearlessly stepping over the missing blocks and emerged into a beautiful night that was the apotheosis of my love. I wandered about, I photographed, I leaned against the merlons for a cigarette, dreaming about this man as I'd never dreamed about Jere. . . . For now I was eight years older, eight years more determined not to lose a second chance. What a lucky woman I was, to have found another right man! How Aunt Agnes would chortle! "It's as I've always said: the world's full of spinsters, and probably every one of 'em came within half an inch of happiness, and lost it by not doing something at the crucial moment. You didn't want to go to Scotland—look what you'd have missed!"

I was on the far side of the fortalice when I heard a pebble rattling somewhere below. I came out of the clouds in a hurry and froze with terror. A rat? Some night animal? I'd nothing for protection against a wildcat, except healthy lungs. Enough noise and perhaps I'd scare an animal into retreat. I shrank into the shadows and strained my ears—would I hear soft paws? There was an agonizing silence, and wary motion. . . .

Human motion . . . a quiet step followed by deliberate wait, then another step. . . .

I knew . . . still I stole forward to peek down.

The Laird was sliding upward against the stone walls. There was a gun in his hand. I was at the edge behind him; he hadn't seen me. I positioned the camera and got a picture; it would be quite clear with the moonlight striking across his grim face. I rolled away and stood up to hang the camera soundlessly on one of the rusty projections behind a merlon.

Where could I hang myself?

Even if I circled around as he emerged, I'd never get down those crumbling stairs without breaking my neck.

Exactly what he wanted. . . .

That gun was not for shooting, but only to knock me out for long enough to toss me from the fortalice, where my shattered body would be discovered tomor-

201

row amid groans over Sable's passion for photography.

Silently I assessed the lower side of the fortalice; it was still more than I thought I could survive . . . and if I had tried to land in a heap with a broken leg, David would come down to finish me off in such a way as to make it seem accidental.

I could scream.

I wouldn't be heard. Strathmuir was asleep. Even if my voice permeated any slumber, it wouldn't create real wakefulness before David knocked me out. If I'd meant to scream, I should have started when I first knew he was on the stairs. He must be nearly at the top by now.

Well, whatever he did to me, someone might find the camera . . . someone might have the film developed and prove murder.

I looked again at the distance to the ground, and it was still too much . . . but there was the projection of the beams holding the top.

Twenty-four square inches. . . .

I crawled between the merlons and somehow got myself onto the thing. Holding onto the edge of the crenel, I hid my face against the stone. It was hopeless, of course. He knew I was here. He'd walk around until he found me. Then he'd simply dislodge me, and I've have a broken neck. I had actually made it easier for him. Oh, how stupid can you be? I was so busy being in love with love, so sure all would be happiness forever. . . .

I could hear him moving about, whispering, "Sable? Sable, luv, where are you?"

In the distance an eerie voice called, "James Cahir?

202

Jamie! Come awa' doon, ye murderer . . ."

I sensed him moving into shadows, knew the gun I couldn't see was poised. Again the voice, Sholto's voice, rang out clear and implacable this time: "James Cahir, come down!" I could hear firm footsteps ascending steadily, and I knew Sholto was first.

He would be.

He was born a Laird, and Laird always leads.

I couldn't stand any more. "Watch out, he's got a gun!" I screamed at the top of my lungs. Something stung across my hand—I hardly felt it in the rush of steps, interchange of shots, unfamiliar voices, and finally Sholto's frantic demand: "Sable? Where are ye, lass?"

"Please, I'm over here, but I can't seem to get up again."

He got me up and into his arms, where upon I looked at him fiercely and said, "You are going to marry me, and we are going to have at least four children: Hamish, Sandy, Chloe and Agnes." After which I had a very comfortable fit of hysterics.

He agreed distractedly, "Yes, yes, anything ye say, so long as ye're safe. Will you stop laughing?"

"Slap her, lad!" Lord Everard's voice directed from below. "'Tis always the action for females in high-strikes. Slap her hard."

Sholto slapped me hard, so hard that I put my hand to my cheek, and he said, "My God, ye're bleeding!"

I was vaguely aware of being swung up and carried down to where Lord Everard was stumping back and forth, irascible with relief. "Dammit, lass, why must ye be wandering about when we'd done our best to protect ye from yon murderer?"

"Not now, Everard! He's winged her—for God's sake where's the doctor? Put the arm up to my shoulder, sweetheart." He was still carrying me, moving sure-footed down the hill with the Lord Lieutenant hobbling swiftly behind.

Lord Everard grumbled anxiously, "Damn the child, I practically put her to bed mysel'—whyfor does she arise?"

"Sholto, I thought you'd gone to Comynhaugh, I was going after you," I wept, "but I didn't know the road and everyone was in bed—so I went to take pictures, and I was loving you so much I forgot him."

"Shhh, be quiet, lass, we're nearly there." He turned sideways, swung through the door to the solarium. "Where's the doctor?" The place was fully lighted. Andrew held the door and lent an arm to Lord Everard. Through my tears I saw quite a tableau: John Morrisy, two men with guns, Lord Camber in a bathrobe, looking very alert, Annis weeping against his shoulder, and a large man opening a black bag, moving toward me.

In the center: the Laird, his left arm suspended, useless in a rough sling of silk scarf.

For a long moment his cold gray eyes met mine. "So you got him," he said, half-smiling in admiration. "Eh, you *were* a clever little luv, Sable."

"He was all I wanted. Oh, David—or whoever you are—why did you?" I asked desperately. "I'd never have said a word."

"No, you never have said a word," he agreed. "You never said your rich aunt had met Mary Kirby, had a picture of her. You never said a word when I was fool enough to show my mother's picture." He laughed. "You praised me for what I'd done for the Clan! You'll never know the hard work—and all the while you meant to destroy it."

"No, I didn't!" I was scarcely aware of the doctor stripping back my sleeve, dousing me with something wet and painful, swiftly bandaging me and using my scarf for a sling. "I didn't care who you were. I thought perhaps you were an illegitimate Gordon who stepped in to maintain the title, and I knew you had worked hard—"

"You thought my mother . . ." Before anyone could catch him, he'd broken forward and knocked me sideways with a sweep of his right arm. I landed in a heap on the couch, while he leaned over me, raving, "I'm no part of your damned Gordons, I've my mother's wedding lines to prove it. How dare you call me a bastard? It was Kirby was the bastard, damn him, damn him!" He slapped me again before the men could drag him away.

Sholto pulled me into his arms. "Get him out of here," he said harshly. "I'd not have brought her this way but I thought ye were gone. Get rid of him!"

"No . . . he didn't do anything to me. Oh, David— I'm sorry. . . ."

"You should be," he remarked venomously. "You'll marry Sholto and step into everything *I* spent twenty years to build. May it make you happy!" With lightning speed, his right hand wrenched the gun from a guard. He put it to his temple and pulled the trigger.

I wound up in Andrew's arms. For a second we clung together, trembling, listening to Annis's screams. Then he turned me to the garden door. "Come away, lass." I stumbled along beside Andrew through the dark paths, and I could not stop sobbing. "I never meant this, I only wanted to know who he was . . . I never asked John to come, or bring anyone. . . . Oh, Andrew, he worked so hard, and it wasn't even his family! Annis loved him, Andrew, even if he had a mistress in Liverpool and drank too much. . . ."

"Hush, child. Mind the step."

"I can't hush. I'd have got him the money from Aunt Agnes for the food packaging. I know he'd have made a brilliant success of it . . . I didn't care who he was . . . oh, why didn't he wait?" We went into a strange room, where Andrew switched on a light, swiftly found a pair of pajamas and turned down the bed. "This isn't the morning room."

"Nay, 'tis Lord Aboyne's quarters, but he'll no' use them tonight. Undress yoursel', lass." Andrew went off to light the bathroom, find a fresh towel, while I tried to open buttons and snaps with one hand. He came back, to strip off my clothes and insert me into pjs as though I were two years old.

"Oh, Andrew, if only I'd never come! I killed him, I'm a murderess. . . ."

"Nay, he killed himsel', as he'd ha' killed you, could he have found ye," Andrew said grimly. "Hush now, child. Into bed, and here's a wee pill the doctor left for ye." Obediently I downed the pill and crawled into bed. Closing my eyes, I could feel covers being tucked around me. The lights turned off, Andrew stood in the doorway. "Think proud of yoursel' for this night, mistress," he said quietly. "No matter how hard he worked, he was no Gordon. Go to sleep and leave the rest to your man."

Chapter 13

Was Sholto my man? True that he'd saved my life. He had said he'd marry me; he would have agreed to anything at that moment. How would he feel now? No matter what Andrew said, my meddling had made Annis a widow. Automatically, Sholto became the Marquess of Huntly, Laird o'Gordon. How could he marry me and set me in her place?

I had no more tears left, I could only lie in the darkness numbly facing the fact that Sholto would not want me now—until finally the sleeping pill knocked me out. . . .

It was nearly noon when I awoke. I heard someone running water in the bathroom and absorbed the significance of my black jacket-dress from which the bright green collar and belt had been removed. . . . Yes, I should wear mourning, sackcloth and ashes for stupidity.

Nellie came out of the bathroom. "I hoped ye'd wake by yourself," she smiled soberly. "Will ye bathe while I bring breakfast? Ye're needed below."

"I'm not hungry. Just coffee, please." I climbed into the bath, gingerly investigated the arm bandages and found the wound was mostly a long, vicious, scraping burn along the forearm. It would itch like fury in another day but was already healing. My hand had got the worst of it, but I could still use it: he hadn't got a vital bone or nerve. Not easy to bathe with one hand, but finally I was done, out and into underclothing. I used the makeup from the case someone had brought from the morning room—but nothing could disguise the dark circles under my eyes.

Nellie came back with a tray and Lady Catherine. "I had to see for myself you were all right," she said, inspecting me keenly. There was sincere concern in her eyes.

"You know it's impossible to kill a Gordon Red!" I looked at the tray. "Oh, Nellie, I only wanted coffee. I can't—"

"But you can and you must, Sable. I will have a cup of coffee, too, Nellie," Lady Catherine stated regally, sinking into a chair and lighting a cigarette. "Sit down, Sable."

Silently, I took a tasteless bite of muffin, sipped coffee. "Annis?" I asked presently.

"Mrs. Cahir has gone to her family home at Rhynie," she said, flicking ashes neatly into a tray. "The guests have left, aside from those directly concerned. Finish your breakfast, Sable."

I finished. I had no idea what I ate. I stood up, Nellie took away the robe and zipped me into the black dress, easing the jacket over my bandaged arm, and fashioning a sling from a black silk scarf.

Finally I was downstairs. As we walked into a

crowded room, everyone rose politely. Lady Catherine pushed me forward, before going to a seat beside Lady Jean on the outskirts. "Ye'll sit here, mistress." Andrew established me next to Lord Everard on the couch, brought out a table with cigarettes, matches, ashtray, and produced a small breakfast pot of coffee.

John Morrisy stood over me, holding my hand anxiously. "The wound? Should it be dressed before we get down to business, Sable?"

I shook my head. "It was only a scrape, already healing." I could see Lord Camber, Lord Atherton in the background, Lawson looking worried, a police stenographer unobtrusively set up in a corner, Morrisy returning to his chair facing me . . . a couple of obvious CID assistants . . . Andrew furnishing ashtrays and matches. . . .

Where was Sholto? Conspicuous by his absence. So I had my answer. I looked at John Morrisy. "Why did you come? I only asked you to identify the prints and tell Lord Everard."

"So I did," he nodded, "I came because the prints were those of a murderer—never convicted, but known as a killer, Sable. There was no way to take you away without tipping our hand—and he'd already had a go at you, but Lord Aboyne and Lord Everard thought they could guard you. Didn't seem likely he'd try again during the party, and we hoped to avert a major scandal."

So the entire display of reels, flings, high spirits, kisses in the garden, were only to prevent scandal? "I see. You were here all the time, then?"

John shook his head. "We drove up from Aberdeen, got here about midnight. Perhaps we should have told you then, Sable, but Lord Aboyne said all had gone so well . . . Nellie said you were abed, locked in. . . . We had a guard to post as soon as the lights were out. We were so nearly home-free, we chanced waiting until the place cleared today," he sighed ruefully, "but you'd already slipped out! We couldn't see you on the hillside from Lord Aboyne's rooms, but you must have been clear as daylight from the Master Chamber. He came down the hall in such a hurry, he nearly caught the guard! We'd been expecting him to force your door, if anything. By the way, I wish you would tell me what in hell you were doing," John demanded forcefully, "with no apology for my language."

"She was choosing names for our four children," Sholto said, over my shoulder. "She had determined to marry me, and the notion had a bit gone to her head."

"Understandable," Lord Camber murmured. "May we ask our questions, gentlemen?"

"Mine first, please. Who was he?" I could sense Sholto standing at the couch behind me; I wouldn't look. Enough to have lost him—why must he shame me publicly with my adolescent sentimentality? God, when I thought of myself, prancing around in the moonlight . . . planning a nursery for a man who'd only kissed me because it was one way to prevent a family scandal!

John Morrisy opened a folder. "His name was James Cahir. . . ." I sat, listening to John's official, toneless voice, and I'd been uncannily right: the Laird *was* a left-handed Englishman, born in 1909 near Liverpool. His mother was a parlormaid, his father a coachman killed at Ypres, and James was a problem—principally because he had a mother complex and forever wanted to make things easier for her. Petty thefts, runner for criminal gangs, but he had always avoided being sent to reform school for lack of evidence.

"He was at sea, wasn't he, on the Atlantic run?"

Morrisy looked up from the folder. "How did you know?"

"He understood my name—and other things."

"He went to sea in 1925; in ten years no firm would hire him," John went on. "Every captain said Cahir was the best man afloat—and a terror ashore. He was bailed out of every jail in every port. Then he learned to kill: a purser vanished overboard . . . a stewardess drowned in Bermuda . . . a rich stupid woman dead of sleeping pills, nothing disturbed, just a jewel case missing. . . . I won't waste time on the others. Nothing could be proved, but every one of the people had had a link to Cahir." John turned a page in the folder.

"When he could no longer get a job at sea, he drifted: driving a truck, petty thievery—again, never proved. The second war put him in the Army, where his bunkmate and eventual buddy was David Kirby. Kirby was a young punk, to whom Cahir was a hero for his, uh, derring-do."

I nodded absently. "Thievery'd appeal to his gypsy blood."

There was a slight pause. "Later," Lord Camber directed. "Go on, Morrisy."

"That's it: Cahir knew everything about Kirby, including the notification of inheritance." John closed the folder. "All the rest is conjecture."

I looked at my toes and felt everyone looking at me . . . but in a way I was admiring James Cahir. "He switched ID tags at Anzio and shot himself in the right

211

arm to explain discrepancy in handwriting," I said slowly. "He was one of the adrenalin kids. He functioned best under pressure. They say practically all clever criminals could be equally successful if they went straight." I looked at John. "Did he kill David Kirby?" I asked suddenly. "He'd have thought the inheritance meant money, and he didn't know his mother was already dead."

"The medical records on the supposed James Cahir show a head wound, as well as severe spinal damage. If he'd lived, he'd have been a hopeless cripple," John said expressionlessly. "Your turn, Sable. I know it was terrifying, but we must have whys and wherefores."

I had been so absorbed in the facts and their significance, I'd half-forgotten the ramifications . . . until I caught a whiff of lavender, glimpsed a sun-browned, graceful hand reaching to flick ashes into my tray. . . .

But he was only waiting, like everyone else, for my explanation of the holocaust. I sat up very straight and began: "Annis made a mistake when she wrote that I could come. He would have put me off, but I was staying with the Campbells, and he wanted to ingratiate himself with the Lord Lieutenant. I expect he assumed I was sixtyish if I were a friend of yours," I said to Lord Everard, who nodded in thoughtful agreement.

"I knew it was a mistake and that nobody really wanted me here, as soon as I came down for dinner the first night. But I thought I'd be through in one day with the records, take a few photographs to please Aunt Agnes, and leave. Then," I said evenly, "Lord Aboyne lured me into describing Mrs. Ware's wealth at dinner.

I expect he knew of her, but obviously the Laird didn't . . . and as he'd been uncooperative about answering her letters in the past . . . well, vulgar or not, I thought I'd let him know what he'd missed," I said apologetically. "I laid it on a bit thick—although there's nothing you could say that'd be too thick about Aunt Agnes's money . . . but he latched onto it at once. He had a scheme . . . probably pretty good . . . and he planned a big party for me that would impress Aunt Agnes so she'd lend him the money."

"Why did you think something was wrong, Sable?"

"Tiny things," I said slowly. "Lady Jean said he had damp hands, and he did—but why should he have the nervous perspiration of someone unable to cope after twenty years of proving himself? Why had no one been admitted to the record room after 1938? Why was he relieved I wanted only late Victorian data? Why didn't he want me left alone at the files for a second? The first day he was breathing down my neck. The next day it was Lord Aboyne. So I thought they were in cahoots to prevent my discovering—something."

Lord Everard cut across the explosive sputtering behind me. "Hush ye, lad!" he said irritably. "What could ye discover?"

"Carmela. Aunt Agnes had said he didn't seem anxious to recall it, and if you aren't somebody, you don't want ancestors who were even less," I said confusedly. "I'm afraid I'm not explaining it very well."

"On the contrary," Lord Camber said, "you're absolutely illuminating! But why should Lord Aboyne connive for such a small thing, Sable?"

"Because he doesn't mind a Gaiety Girl grand-mother, but if the Laird were embarrassed by a Spanish

213

gypsy, Lord Aboyne would say nothing," I said simply, "and anyway, it wasn't a small thing, except that I didn't know enough about your laws to realize it."

"I never even heard of a gypsy," Sholto protested violently.

"Yes, well, I fancy that is the crux of the situation," Lord Camber murmured, "and Sable is going to tell us about her."

"The first David Kirby married one during the Peninsular Wars; Wellington himself was a witness." I looked confidingly at Lord Camber. "Then Kirby was killed, a year later the girl turned up here, complete with child and marriage papers. Aunt Agnes had said here was a diary she hadn't had time to finish . . . but it all added up to some sort of fun-gossip, and I was so mad at all this chaperonage, I was determined to dig it out to amuse Aunt Agnes. Not nice of me, I suppose—but when they so obviously didn't want me, even while the Laird was trying to use me for money . . . and someone was reading my daily diary for Aunt Agnes and steaming open my letter to the Campbells—" I looked apologetically at Lord Camber, ignoring the choked gasp behind me—"I sort of lost my temper."

Lord Camber's eyes opened sharply, but he only nodded.

"Well, they thought I'd gone to Aberdeen for a dress, but Annis gave me some silk for Nellie to make up, so I had a free morning. I concentrated on the gypsy . . . and there were *two* baby boys. The illegitimate one looked like his father; the wedlock baby looked 'most unfortunately' like Carmela. Their names were George and David. Once Carmela left with a Romany caravan, the family loved them dearly. A year later, George died." Now the room was electric with suspense.

"Nothing anywhere said which child was which," I finished. "There's one letter marked on the file card 'discarded as illegible' in 1935. That's the one that identified the children, of course, but Cahir couldn't delete *all* references to two children without leaving a suspicious gap. Especially as Huntly records were known to be particularly well documented."

"My God," Morrisy muttered involuntarily, "what a spot to be in! He found that he not only had to conceal imposture but also that Kirby had no right to the title in the first place!"

"But I didn't know that. I thought it was like—oh, having a horse-thief on an American family tree. When Lord Everard explained, I expect it showed in my face. Both the Laird and Lord Aboyne looked grim."

"I felt grim," Sholto's voice remarked. "Everard's case involves an old friend. Go on, cousin—I'm eager to know why you supposed I would aid an impostor."

"Death duties. I thought perhaps they were bilking the tax collector to save Clan properties," I said with the clarity of rage. If he hadn't the guts to come out and face me, let him take it between the eyes! "The Laird said he wouldn't explain the financial arrangements, except that they were advantageous to both of them. Lord Aboyne already had land and titles, and the Laird didn't have a son—the succession would automatically get back where it belonged when he died."

"Good Heavens!" Lord Everard muttered, awed, while the others burst into laughter.

"A fertile feminine explanation if I ever heard one," Morrisy chuckled.

I felt ashamed of my temper. "I'm—sorry. . . ."

"Nay, don't apologize, cousin. Your estimate of ma character is verra . . . revealing, so say naught of your own," Sholto snorted. "Gypsies, horse-thieves, tax bilkers—nothing bothers ye!"

I hung my head unhappily, until Lord Camber said gently, "Go on, please: how did you know he wasn't Kirby?"

"He showed me a picture of his mother the night he got drunk in the record room, and I knew it wasn't Mary Kirby. Aunt Agnes has a wedding picture of George and Mary Kirby."

Camber sat up like a jack-in-the-box. "He didn't know that?"

I shook my head. "He was an opportunist, I thought he'd—oh, try to use it somehow, hearts and flowers, auld lang syne. So I didn't say anything at first, and later. . . . Well, he had gray eyes; George and Mary Kirby had brown eyes. He *might* have been a throwback to the bastard who would have had light eyes if he looked like his father . . . but when I saw the picture, it was another woman entirely."

The room was silent, intent. "I couldn't think what best to do," I went on, forcing my voice to steadiness. "You see, I still thought there might be an explanation; perhaps he was an illegitimate Gordon who thought Lord Aboyne was dead, too, so he stepped in to maintain the title. Things can get confused in wartime. Finally, I sent the guest list to John, to check fingerprints . . . and I expect I haven't a very good character," I finished in a small voice, "because if he'd been a Gordon, I'd never have said a word. He said he found nothing when he took over. Whatever there is now, it's what he built, and why wouldn't he enjoy it?

216

He must have worked very hard."

"Too right!" Lawson grunted emphatically.

"The last thing I meant was to rock the boat," I whispered. "I knew he tried to kill me in the blind; I thought it was the entail, and I figured out a red herring: I pretended to think him worried that the old Laird was a byblow of Edward VII."

"WHAT?"

"No, no," I said hastily, "just a tale to explain my shock. I gambled that he wouldn't be able to find the diary I was talking about and compare the dates until after I had left for the Campbells'. He seemed so convinced, that I was fooled—but he wasn't one to take a chance on anyone but himself."

"No," Lord Camber agreed, "and he probably was convinced you didn't understand the entail problem, but," he smiled faintly, "after you went upstairs, Cargill sentimentally spilled the beans. He had driven your aunt to Liverpool, to visit a relative the day after she was here for that houseparty. Cargill explained that Agnes had met Mary Kirby, and Cahir picked it up at once."

Lord Camber glanced around the room. "Well, I think that ends it, gentlemen . . . although I cannot refrain from saying it would have been better handled if you or Morrisy had given me your confidence, Everard. Sable would then have moved into my wife's room, never been offered the hot chocolate, let alone been permitted to traipse in the moonlight. . . ."

I caught my breath as I remembered the bitter taste and Annis's white face. I hardly heard Lord Camber say: "However, she's safe, if no thanks to you." He stood up, smiling at me. "Thank you for making the effort when you must be so tired, my dear. You're a very gallant young woman." He patted my hand kindly. "Cathy, if you're ready? Lawson, will you carry on pro tem?"

Lawson nodded curtly. "What do we say?" A long silence. . . .

"A tragic accident with his hunting gun," I said. "Whoever, whyever, however, the man spent twenty years coping. You've agreed he did well. I don't care how many people he killed when he was young. He didn't kill me. He deserves that much decent recognition for going straight . . . to say nothing of Annis who loved him, as well as the woman in Liverpool," I added distractedly. "I expect she loved him, too, and what's to become of them?"

"Not my affair," Lady Catherine observed, "but I agree—to say nothing. I'm ready when you are, Charles." She leaned over to kiss me. "Goodbye, Sable, until we meet again."

Dumbly, I sat on the couch . . . watching Lady Catherine leave; shaking hands politely with Lord Atherton and with the two large gentlemen who turned out to be Liverpool police and War Office; watching the police stenog removing himself discreetly, Andrew emptying ashtrays impassively.

John Morrisy held my hand briefly. "Have to race for the Aberdeen plane, Sable, but you were a trump! Put the whole thing out of your mind for a while," he said authoritatively. "That's an order! We'll be looking for you when you get back to London."

It was finished; everyone was going away. Lawson came toward me. "How did you know about Mavis?"

"Is that her name? I didn't know, it just—figured."

He nodded. "I told him you were smarter than he thought," he remarked. "When the smoke clears, I'd appreciate your backing me to take over."

I ignored it. "Mavis? Did he provide for her at all? Is she a good secretary, can she get another job?"

"Easily. I'd keep her myself, if she'd stay." He looked at the floor. "God, I dread telling her," he burst out. "Too right she loved him! Enough to do without a wedding ring when he decided the smart move was Annis."

Twenty years a mistress? "I see. Well, it's scant comfort, but I expect he thought of her as his real wife. Do your best for her, Alf."

"I will," he said somberly. "I suppose you did what you thought right, but there are those who won't agree, Miss Lennox."

Too right, as he'd have said himself. And Sholto, Lord of Aboyne, Sutherland and Gordon, now speeding the remnants of the conference through the hall, was evidently among them. I took a last look at my love and went out to the garden. I suddenly remembered: my handbag with all essential papers was in the car where I'd left it when I had gone to the fortalice. The hell with luggage; let them forward it . . . or throw it away. . . .

All I wanted was to get out of here. Now!

I couldn't.

Sandy was bringing out the other cars; he'd pulled mine to the rear and blocked it with the estate jeep, while he maneuvered Lord Camber's Aston-Martin down the drive. There were still some police-ish MGs, a battered Renault and the Campbell's Sunbeam, with a crumpled fender Lord Everard wouldn't replace, "the way it'll remind ma wife not to tangle wi' a herd o' cattle again."

There was no way to free my car. Probably better to wait until the rest were gone, anyway. I went into the stable section and sat with Jennie while the pups were having a snack. Finally I heard Sandy moving the jeep back into its stall and departing with a blithe whistle toward the kitchen. Peering at my watch in the dimness, I could see it was nearly four; Sandy was going down for staff tea. I could leave now . . . and where was I to go?

Would any hotel take me in without luggage? Strathbogie would have the news by now, and I couldn't face questions or curiosity from the Mac-Danalds. The Campbells wouldn't want me, either. Could I drive to Aberdeen, leave the car and fly back to London? The Morrisys would take me in until I could get passage for New York. Yes, that was best.

Drearily, I pulled myself out of the shadows and crawled into the car. The Renault and the Sunbeam were still there, but I could get past them with a little care. I settled the driving pillow, started the engine and made for the front court; I had to back and position the car to wiggle between the others, but at last I was through . . . then I saw Andrew sprinting across ahead of me. He stood directly in my path, hands on hips, yelling, "EeeeeeoooooHEEEEEEE!"

Instantly, Sholto came leaping down the steps, with the Campbells and Lord Atherton right behind him. He leaned through the car window and practically wrenched the key from the ignition. "And waur d'ye think ye're going now?" he demanded vehemently.

"I'm leaving. I was always to leave today—and I'll

thank you for the key to my car."

Sholto threw it over his shoulder, opened the driver's door and bodily plucked me forth. "Ye'll never have another," he informed me. "Waur have ye been, ye silly clunch? Here's the whole house roused to hunt, in and out of every room, Cathy and Charles delayed, waiting as long as possible, worried to death . . . and here ye come," he snorted furiously, "fresh as the breeze, just stepping out for a wee trip!"

"To Aberdeen for the next London plane. Please let me go."

"Wi' no luggage? And why for London, when ye're bespoke for my godfather," he said, bewildered, "the way ye'll stay here till all's settled." His hands tightened on my shoulders. "Did ye or did ye not tell me at dawn this day ye meant to marry me?" I gulped and stared fixedly at his middle coat button. "Ye promised me four children: Hamish, Sandy, Chloe and Agnes," he said, "and I agreed to all of it—forbye ye may expect more of me than I can perform at ma advanced age, but ye've got me anxious to try."

The others chuckled, and Andrew made a most unbutlerish snort. My eyes filled with tears, as a warm hand forced my chin up.

"I love you, well you know it," Sholto said quietly. "Last night you cared nothing for fifteen years. Has your mind changed with daylight?" His lips twisted sadly. "If ye dinna care to marry an evil-tempered old man—why, say so, cousin, and there's an end of it."

"I love you with all my heart—but after this terrible mess, how can you marry me?"

"You and no other, dear heart," he assured me tenderly. When I came up for air, the courtyard was tactfully empty. "Come away in, darling—or will it distress you to stay here?" he asked, suddenly troubled. "The Campbells will bear ye company, but I'll take ye to Comynhaugh and Bessie, if ye'd prefer."

"I'll stay wherever you are going to stay, please."

It was not too difficult, after all, with so much to do. Lord Everard kept me busy over the files for an hour, and eventually I found what the Laird had missed: a schoolgirl's diary thirty years later, with a reference to the unexpected—and definitely unwanted—return of the Kirby bastard. "Uncle Sandy and papa gave him some money," wrote Miss Amelia, "and told him to go away again as there was young ladies in the house. Jane and me had a sight of him from the landing—a great ruffianly fellow in coarse clothing, but the image of his father's portrait that hangs in the gallery. I think his eyes were even bluer."

"That settles it," Lord Everard said, closing the book with a sigh of satisfaction. "Let's have tea."

As I washed in the powder room, I wondered where I was to sleep? Not in Annis's room! Clinging sickly to the hand bowl, I wondered where Sholto and I would live. Would we use the Master Chamber . . . ? *Put it out of your mind for a while, that's an order!*

I put it out of my mind, dried my hands and emerged to face Mrs. Frame, who was obviously lying in wait. "The Lady Jean has said ye should return to your first room," she reported. "The luggage has been transported back. The other rooms have been light-cleaned, that way they're orderly until we've time. The Lady Jean has said ye should no' be bothered wi' details this day, we'd use our judgment for dinner, but I'll appreciate a moment tomorrow for your instructions, the way I'll know how to go on hereafter."

Such instant acceptance was—unnerving. "Thank you, Mrs. Frame—breakfast time, perhaps?"

She nodded dismissingly; something still to be said? She took a firm breath, "And the staff directs me to tell ye we'll have a pleasure in serving ye, milady, do ye care to retain us."

"I'm sure Lord Aboyne has no thought of change," I said shakily, "and I'm not milady."

"Ye will be," she returned blandly. "Och, aye, we knew from the first day. When Andrew came down from depositing your luggage. 'Here's the one for Master Sholto,' he tell't us. 'A Gordon Red she is, and already he canna tell his head from his hand!' Och, aye," she nodded merrily, "ye'll suit him, milady. Some grand clishmaclavers there'll be, the way life'll be exciting once more . . . and Nellie has a young sister just ready to be nursemaid in a twelvemonth," she finished comfortably. "Go along to your tea, now. . . ."

The room was empty. Inevitably I was drawn to the window, and the fortalice was still kindly and protective in itself . . . but someone would have to go up and retrieve the camera I'd left on a spike. It couldn't be me. I'd never be able to go up those steps again, except in all-too-vivid memory. I was unconsciously clenching my hands together, staring at the tower and somehow mentally there, crouched on one of the projections. If Sholto hadn't come . . . ?

With a metallic rattle, the long draperies swirled across the windows, shutting out the view. "Come away, beloved," Sholto said, taking me into his arms.

223

Behind him I could see the Campbells and the Athertons disposing themselves about the tea table.

Lord Everard eyed me commandingly, his shaggy eyebrows very straight and firm. "Once and for all, Sable," he stated. "'Twas no fault o'yours. The man chose his own road, not once but twice. He gambled, he lost."

Lady Jean was calmly pouring tea. "Edgar, are you taking sugar or not? Everard, here you are, dear. Rose, may I have the cucumber sandwiches?" It was quite calm and peaceful; it was going to have to be that way, and I would have to adjust to it, because Lord Everard was right.

James Cahir had chosen his own path, had set it in the shadows and had chosen not to face sunlight and clear air.

True, I'd created the need for a choice—but I had not made it for him. I sensed Sholto waiting quietly for me to gain perspective.

"Have your tea, my dear," Lady Jean was saying, "and tell us about the wedding."

I slid my hand through Sholto's arm and went forward. "We'd better discuss the wedding," I remarked, "because the staff is already training Nellie's young sister for nursemaid."